THE
SLEEPING
BAOBAB
TREE

Paula Leyden was born in Kenya and spent her childhood in Zambia. As a teenager she moved with her family to South Africa, where she soon became involved in the struggle to end Apartheid. Since 2003 she has lived on a farm in Kilkenny, Ireland, with her partner and five children, where she breeds horses and writes. *The Sleeping Baobab Tree* is Paula's second novel, sequel to the Éilís Dillon Award-winning *The Butterfly Heart*.

Withdrawn from Stock
Dublin City Public Libraries

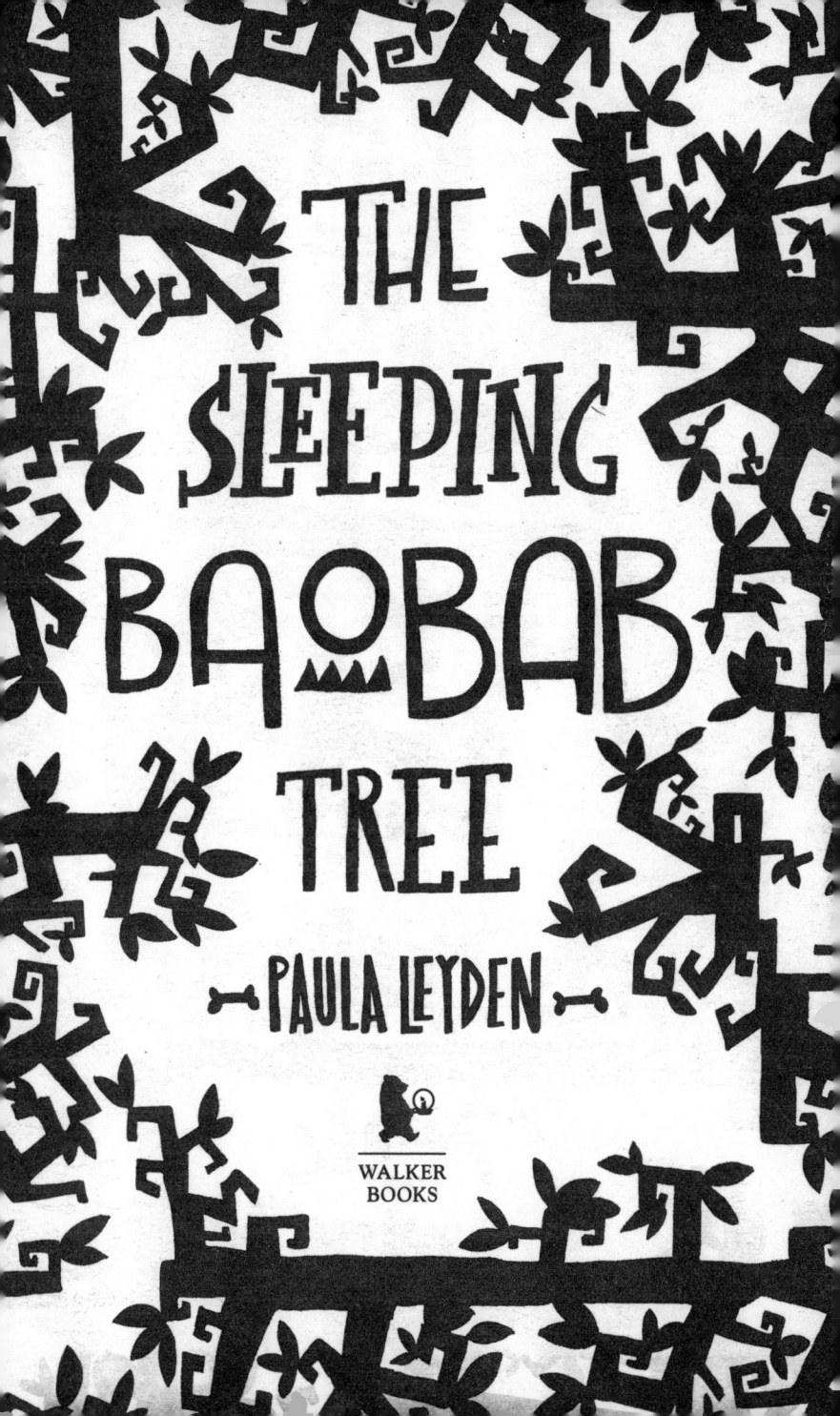

THE SLEEPING BAOBAB TREE

~ PAULA LEYDEN ~

WALKER
BOOKS

This is a work of fiction. Names, characters, places and incidents
are either the product of the author's imagination or, if real, are used
fictitiously. All statements, activities, stunts, descriptions, information
and material of any other kind contained herein are included for
entertainment purposes only and should not be relied on for
accuracy or replicated, as they may result in injury.

First published 2013 by Walker Books Ltd
87 Vauxhall Walk, London SE11 5HJ

2 4 6 8 10 9 7 5 3 1

Text © 2013 Paula Leyden
Cover and interior illustrations © 2013 Gillian Hibbs

The right of Paula Leyden to be identified as the author of this
work has been asserted by her in accordance with the
Copyright, Designs and Patents Act 1988

This book has been typeset in Bembo, Kosmik Bold and Dink Scratch

Printed and bound in Great Britain by Clays Ltd, St Ives plc

All rights reserved. No part of this book may be reproduced,
transmitted or stored in an information retrieval system in any
form or by any means, graphic, electronic or mechanical,
including photocopying, taping and recording, without prior
written permission from the publisher.

British Library Cataloguing in Publication Data:
a catalogue record for this book is available from the British Library

ISBN 978-1-4063-2793-9

www.walker.co.uk

This book is for Dad, Mum, Julia, John and Karen, with love

Pembroke Branch Tel. 6689575

BUL - BOO

Bukoko the Little Tick Child

In a side pocket of my rucksack I have a small red notebook. It's where we (i.e. Madillo my twin sister, Fred our neighbour and me, of course) note down what happens at school. Or more specifically what happens in Sister Leonisa's class. She's our religion teacher. There are three columns on each page: GOD, STORY, WORK. It's different from my small black notebook, where I write down the things that I think about. That belongs to just me.

In the GOD column we fill in how often Sister mentions God, and most days we write "zero". Sister Leonisa says that talking about God all the time can get boring.

In the STORY column we put a tick if she tells us a story and a sad face if she doesn't. Well, Madillo puts a sad face, I just put an X. I'm not big on sad or smiley faces.

Most of that column is ticked.

The WORK column is the emptiest – if we ever get to do any work in her class she never takes it in anyway, so it doesn't really count.

I decided that we should start the book because I like keeping records of things. You never know when you might need something as evidence. I'd hate to be called as a witness before a judge and have to look down in an embarrassed kind of way and say, "Sorry, Your Honour, I can't remember anything."

Madillo says it's not strictly necessary, because Sister Leonisa hasn't committed a crime so we don't need evidence. "Not yet," I tell her. "There's plenty of time."

As soon as Sister walked into the classroom today I knew we could tick the STORY column, leave the WORK one blank and put a big zero underneath GOD. She said just two words as she stepped through the door: "Zebras down!"

The Zebras are the blinds she made from old sheets. She said we could use them because the rest of the nuns had outgrown them.

As if an adult can outgrow a sheet.

I asked Sister how this was possible and she said, "There are many things you don't know about nuns, Bul-Boo." Which is no kind of answer at all. What's not to know about nuns? That they grow mysteriously in

the night and then reshape themselves back to normal size in the morning?

Sister Leonisa never says, "I don't know." She hates admitting to not knowing something, so instead she makes up answers.

Madillo (who also likes having an answer for everything) says it must be because the nuns eat so much that they are all getting fat, but one look at Sister Leonisa would tell you that's not true. She looks just like one of the matchstick drawings she does on the blackboard.

Anyway, the blinds are called Zebras because Sister got us to paint black stripes on them before she hung them up. She said the sun would be hurt if we shut it out completely – that's why we left the strips of white. She talks about things like the sun as if they have feelings.

In Sister's world, the sun is a woman. An angry woman if you put up blinds to shut her out. So we have stripy ones which let in half the light and don't work very well if we are watching a DVD but do work for stories.

So we rolled them down.

Once they were down she started.

"Ng'ombe Ilede ... Ng'ombe Ilede," she said, her voice deep and rumbling. "The Place of the Sleeping Cow. The place of death."

9

That's another category I should have put into the notebook: **STORIES THAT HAVE DEATH IN THEM**. That column would be ticked all the way down. We never tell Mum and Dad her stories any more, because they say she's morbid. They may be right but we're used to her. I think if she told us a story about pink fairies we'd all leave the room.

"Ng'ombe Ilede is a town crawling with ghosts," Sister said, making crawling movements with her hands. "They sit up in the trees, swim in the warm waters of the Kariba Dam, wait behind old walls. They are everywhere, and they're watching."

There is something about the way Sister Leonisa speaks that makes you believe what she's telling you, even if you don't want to, and even if you know that nearly all of it is exaggerated.

"One of these ghosts is called Bukoko," she continued. "Do you know how she got that name?"

We all shook our heads. By now we know that the only person Sister wants an answer from is herself.

"Because that's what you call a child whose mother drinks too much beer when she's pregnant. Poor little child, sitting there in her mother's stomach, drinking gallons of beer, burping away from all the bubbles. When a baby burps in its mother's stomach the air has nowhere to go, so the poor child gets squashed. This

happened to Bukoko and by the time she came out she was tiny, a small beer-pickled baby. Bukoko the Little Tick Child is what they all called her, because her belly was full and round, like a tick after a good drink of cow's blood."

Along with death, Sister manages to add the gross factor to every story she tells. I sometimes think that if she wanted to tell a story that wasn't gross already she'd just add in a string of disgusting words at the end to satisfy herself.

I put my hand up. "I've never heard of a baby burping inside its mother's stomach. I don't think that's scientifically proven."

I saw Madillo scrunching up her face. She hates it when I use the phrase "scientifically proven", especially in Sister's class.

"Just because some of us have mothers and fathers who are doctors," Sister said, "we think we know everything. But we don't. There are some things that doctors and scientists will never know because they close their minds to them. Now, if I can carry on?

"Poor little Tick grew only one centimetre each year. She grew so slowly that her mother despaired of her. Nothing would work. Every morning after milking the cow her mother would set aside the cream off the top of the milk especially for Bukoko so that she

could grow up into a big strong woman."

Sister rolled her eyes. "Even a man whose eyes had been gouged out by an eagle could have seen that this was never going to happen. But Bukoko was a happy child, her round belly was filled with creamy milk and her little legs were strong. They were able to carry her far and wide, and during the day when her mother wasn't looking she would run off into the nearby forest to play with the Little People."

Surely Sister Leonisa was muddled about this. She's always adding in bits of other stories. Everyone knows that the Little People are from Ireland, not Zambia. Unless there are some who migrated here. Like the Red Legs in Jamaica. Mum told us once that Oliver Cromwell (who seemed to spend his time either killing people, burning down their houses or turning them into slaves) sent some Irish people to Barbados (yup, as slaves) and their descendants stayed there. They became known as Red Legs because they get burnt by the sun, which the Barbadians don't. I think that must be true, because Mum doesn't like the sun, and if by accident she sits in it for too long her legs go red. Anyway, to give Sister the benefit of the doubt, maybe Oliver Cromwell enslaved the Little People from Ireland and sent them all to Zambia. But I'm seriously doubtful.

"Every day Bukoko played happily with her little

friends, until one day," Sister lowered her voice to a ghostly whisper, "one day, the day of her thirteenth birthday, she went into the forest and didn't come back. All the villagers were helpless, weeping and wailing about the loss of their little tick girl. Weeping and wailing never did anyone any good at all. You remember that, girls and boys," Sister added. "Especially if it's fake. Then all it is is a lot of irritating noise.

"Night fell and the darkness crept around the houses in the village. Then the moon rose, bright and full in the sky, and the weepers and wailers went to bed, leaving the poor mother alone outside, calling and calling to her daughter. No sign of Bukoko. But, as midnight struck, the mother heard a little voice she recognized, 'Mama! Mama!' It was her child, Bukoko. But where was the voice coming from?"

Sister looked at us and Madillo, as usual, forgot she wasn't supposed to answer.

"From the forest?" she said.

Sister shook her head. "No, Madillo, how do you think the little tick child could climb a tree on her tiny legs?"

Which was a bit unfair as Madillo hadn't actually said in a *tree* in the forest. But Sister didn't give her a chance to reply.

"The voice came from the sky. The mother looked

up and, by the light of the moon, she saw Bukoko sitting cross legged on a small soft cloud.

"'Come down, my child,' she squawked. 'Right this minute. We are looking for you.'

"Bukoko shook her head. 'No, Mama, I'm not coming down. I like it here. Up here nobody calls me a tick or laughs at me, they all think I'm just a perfect girl. I think this is where I'll stay for ever.'

"And, just like that, *whoosh*, she disappeared. Never to be seen again.

"Her mother fell to the ground and writhed around in anguish. 'Gone, gone for ever, my little girl.'

"As the mother lay there, clouds of dust rising all around her, she started to wonder how she would explain this to the rest of the village. She felt shame creep over her. How could she tell the others that her daughter had left her, of her own free will? That wouldn't do at all.

"So what do you think she did, girls and boys?"

I spoke up. "She shouldn't be worrying about how she was going to explain it – she should still be upset. How could she be thinking about anything else apart from her daughter stuck up on a cloud?" I said. "And anyway, nobody could sit on a cloud, because a cloud is just millions and billions of water droplets – it's like saying she was sitting on a cloud of flour, which is impossible."

"Well, I never said she was going to win Mother

of the Year, did I, Bul-Boo?" Sister replied. "And, as I've said to you many times before, you can't explain everything with science and droplets of water and flour. There are other things in this world that you and I can't see. Magical things. I tell you now, Mrs Scientifically Proven, anything is possible if you just believe it."

She then carried on as if I'd said nothing.

"The mother's clever plan was to pretend that a two-legged hyena had come into the forest and bitten Bukoko's head off so that all that was left of her was her small dead body. So she hurried home and wrapped some of her daughter's clothes around a medium-sized rock and placed this rock in a wooden casket on a bed of grass. She then called all the neighbours and told them her sad tale. Through her tears she explained that they could view the body but the head was gone, into the belly of the hyena. The funeral was held and Bukoko the Rock was buried. There she lay, silently, until one day when the Archaeologists came and dug her up."

Sister said "Archaeologists" as if it was a swear word. In her list of Evil People in the World, archaeologists are right up there near the top.

"So, from the stone in a grave they learnt the whole story?" I asked.

I already knew that trying to debate logically with Sister was futile. But today I couldn't help it.

"On her deathbed the mother confessed to her wicked lie, Bul-Boo, as people do. Her words were repeated and the story was passed down through many centuries until it arrived here today. Now I am passing it on to you and you can pass it on to your children. One day perhaps they will go on a school trip to Ng'ombe Ilede and see the ghost of little Bukoko wandering around happily near the tree called the Sleeping Cow."

The bell rang for break time and she clapped her hands. "Now, no more questions. Enough is enough."

As we were getting up to go I saw Madillo grabbing her skirt pocket. She always forgets to switch off her phone. The problem with that is that even if it's on silent Sister says she can hear a vibrating phone from a mile away. And she can. Luckily this time she didn't because there was such a racket going on around her.

Madillo read her message once we were safely out of Sister's sight. It was from Fred.

"I am having a DOOM day," it said.

I knew straight away why he had sent this to Madillo instead of me. Even though recently Fred has grown taller and deeper-voiced and all that, he still thinks silly things. They never sound silly to Madillo though. She takes all this stuff seriously.

Fred is now convinced that he has gifts. Magical powers inherited from Nokokulu, his great-granny.

"Nokokulu" doesn't actually mean "great-granny", it means "granny', but everyone calls her that anyway. I'm not sure why. Even my family does, and she's not related to us. Anyway, I don't believe there are such things as magical powers and I certainly don't believe Fred has them. One of his gifts, he says, is that he can see into the future – but only the bad future. So when he says DOOM we are all supposed to know that he has had one of his tragic prophecies. He never sees good things. In fact he doesn't see anything in any detail – he gets this big gloom cloud that hangs over his head, and then he knows that sometime in the future something awful is going to befall him. Which is not much of a gift, in my opinion, because we all pretty much know that at some stage in our lives something awful might happen. Well, definitely *will* happen. All his gift is, as I've told him, is that some-times he imagines the worst, then the worst comes true.

Madillo believes in his gifts and is very jealous of them. She has always wanted magical powers.

His text explained why he wasn't at school today. When he has these doom-filled predictions he doesn't even get out of bed in case he falls down the stairs and is left permanently brain-damaged.

I have to say I was feeling pretty doom laden myself. But for different reasons.

FRED

Doom and Gloom

The minute I woke up this morning I knew that everything was going to go wrong. Not just ever-so-slightly wrong but mind-bendingly, end-of-the-world kind of wrong.

How did I know this?

My curse of a gift.

Prediction. Premonition. Foretelling Doom.

To be precise, I can predict *when* things are going to go wrong. It's a sixth or seventh or perhaps ninth sense. The only problem is, it is never *exact*. If it was, I could prevent anything bad ever happening around me. But somehow, when this gift was passed onto me from my wretched great-grandmother, one small bit was left out. The bit that gives the detail.

All I get is the general gloom.

Which is why, so far, I have spent quite a lot of my life in a state of peculiar, all-consuming dread. Predicting awfulness, that's my speciality.

This gift, you see, never forewarns me that everything is going to go absolutely *right*: that all will be well in the world; that (one of) the girls next door will fall hopelessly in love with me, despite the fact that they only think of me as the boy next door; that my marks in school will miraculously improve or that my parents will transform into normal friendly human beings. No. I'm never forewarned of that. Instead I wake up, as I did this morning, with a large dark cloud hovering over me and a sinking feeling of Unstoppable Wrongness crowding my brain.

I lay there for a while, thinking that I must be mistaken. The sun was shining outside my window, the birds were squawking and the sky was blue. I pulled my sheet up over my eyes and waited. After a very long wait I threw back the sheet with my eyes still closed and jumped out of bed in one movement. When I opened my eyes, there I was with my head in the gloomy cloud. Yup, it was still there. If I was able to stand on my head for longer than a few seconds the cloud would shift position and gather round me on the floor. No escaping this one.

So, here I am. Fred, the boy next door.

There will never be a Fred Junior or Fred II or anything like that. The name Fred started with me and so shall it end. If I have to hear another person telling me all the words Fred rhymes with, I may just whack them. They'll be the unlucky one among a thousand wise-cracking jerks who have felt the need to tell me that Fred rhymes with bed, head and dead.

Hi, I'm Fred.

Oh, poor old Fred, he went to bed and woke up dead with a worm in his head.

It's beside the point that if he woke up he wasn't dead anyway.

My second name is Chiti. I won't even talk about what that rhymes with. But it does mean that I was named after the greatest chief that ever lived in Zambia – Chief Chitimukulu, Chiti the Great. I think that was to make up for my first name. I am one hundred per cent certain there were no great chiefs called Fred. Even the two words together sound stupid. Chief Fred. I can't imagine people bowing down before a name like that, unless they were trying to hide the fact that they were laughing.

What I do when I'm surrounded by impending doom clouds is try to imagine what the worst thing is that can happen. Today my imaginings were pretty standard:

I could be swallowed whole by a python after it had slowly and methodically crushed me.

I could be savaged by a pack of hyenas that had run out of things to scavenge.

Worse still, the ancient bone-crushing hyena, with a head bigger than a lion, could come back from extinction with a special mission to hunt me down.

Or I could accidentally sit on a scorpion and die an agonizing, paralysing death. One of those deaths where your tongue sticks out and your face goes purple.

Maybe the worst possibility is what could happen at school. Sister Leonisa is one of our teachers – for the second year in a row – and with her anything can happen.

I reckoned that apart from the scorpion and maybe the python I could avoid all of them by just staying home. The scorpion would be easily avoided by keeping my shoes on all day and never sitting down. The python – well, the python I'd just have to hope would be small enough for me to be able to grab the back of its neck with one hand and the end of its tail with the other. It's been done before. Not by me, but by someone, I'm sure.

Sister Leonisa I would avoid by not going to school.

Now all I had to do was to persuade Mum and Dad that I had to stay home at all costs. Neither of them believed in my gift, so I would have to lie to them.

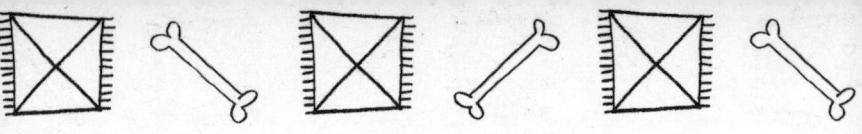

My two best friends, Bul-Boo and Madillo, live next door to me. They're identical twins, but they're not identical in their ways, only what they look like. The three of us have come up with four categories of lies. I think everyone should know them:

Necessary Lies.

Half Lies.

Kind Lies.

Wrong Lies.

The first three categories are allowed. It's only the last one that you should avoid.

So, out of necessity (i.e. to avoid a tragic, painful death) I would have to pretend to be sick.

I'm pretty good at being sick on demand. When I try really hard I'm even able to make myself look pale and ghostly. So when Mum said to me, "Yes, sweetie, go back up to bed, you're looking quite washed out," I knew I'd succeeded, and I stumbled – in a diseased, pasty kind of way – back to bed.

To wait.

And imagine.

BUL-BOO

Professor Ratsberg and Dr Wrath

The reason why today was not a good day for stories about death, or for anything much else for that matter, was the conversation I accidentally overheard last night.

I wasn't really eavesdropping. I was sitting on the stairs writing in my little black notebook, the book I don't share with Madillo and Fred, before going to bed. It was very hot in the bedroom and Madillo was humming an irritating tune, so I had decided to wait on the stairs till Mum came to say goodnight. It was then that I heard them.

"It's happening again," she said.

"What is, Lula?" Dad asked.

"Last week it was Thandiwe's death notice in the paper. Today, Sonkwe's family came to tell me he was

dead too." Her voice sounded ghost-like. "They wanted to know why. Sonkwe had told them that Doctor Lula was going to make sure he had a long life. Because that *is* what I had promised him."

I remembered that voice from before, from the time when Mum's patients were dying one after the other. I thought that had all been fixed. Mum talks to us a lot about her work, more than Dad does, so we know when things are going well. Since she has started receiving a steady supply of medicines, things have been good. She says that as long as she has a year's supply in the clinic, she can keep ahead of herself and her patients will live.

She still worries. She worries about people who can't get to the clinic, people who don't know about the medicines they need, people who won't get an AIDS test. But she doesn't worry as much as she did then, because she says that things are improving all the time.

"If patients decide to stop taking their medication there's nothing you can do," Dad said gently. "It's their decision."

"No, you don't get it," she said. "Sonkwe and Thandiwe would never have done that. I know them. They could see that the medication was working. They wouldn't just stop without talking to me. And don't tell me it's a coincidence," she added, "that they both disappeared from the clinic three months ago."

24

"They did? Stopped coming entirely?" Dad had already forgotten that he was supposed to be consoling her. "Why didn't you follow it up?"

Dad doesn't work in the same HIV/AIDS clinic as Mum any more. He works in an office and is in charge of several clinics. Sometimes I think he forgets that Mum is not his employee.

"I asked the nurses to do it," she said quietly. "I should have done it myself and now it's too late."

"Sorry, Lula," Dad said. "Of course I know you would have had someone follow up. But tell me, has anyone else stopped coming for their check-ups?"

It was a while before Mum answered. Finally she said, "I've looked back and there are eight others who stopped attending at almost exactly the same time. I don't know how I hadn't noticed before."

"There we are," Dad said. "That's not so bad. Only eight out of — how many? You have over a thousand regulars. Eight not showing up is not unusual. People move jobs. Family circumstances change. They could have been going to clinics in other areas."

"You still don't get it," Mum said. "These are ten of our very first patients. That's how I know them all. And Sonkwe's family didn't know he'd stopped attending the clinic, he never told them. Then I made contact with Thandiwe's people and it's the same story. They

thought she was still living in town and coming here for her treatment. Plus, we haven't managed to contact any of the other eight. I'm sure there's something really wrong."

"Don't worry. There'll be a logical explanation."

"*Logical?* Like the time when that so-called 'doctor' came here peddling the pool cleaner Tetrasil as a cure? The same thing happened then. What's worse is, when the other patients hear of them dying, they'll think there's no point taking their own medication and stop. Then we'll be right back to the worst days of the catastrophe."

"Email me the ten names tomorrow," Dad said. "I'll go through them myself. We'll get to the bottom of it. It'll be all right, you'll see."

"No, Sean, it won't. It really won't be all right."

"Wait," Dad said suddenly. "Did you say these were your first patients? Kiki was one of your first patients."

"Yes," Mum replied, so quietly I could hardly hear her. "Kiki had been coming into the clinic, you know that. She'd been helping me there. She wouldn't stop coming without telling me."

I crept away then.

When I got back into bed my head was reeling from what I'd just heard. Aunt Kiki disappeared? Why hadn't Fred told us? Perhaps he didn't know. I wrote in my

black notebook: Aunt Kiki and nine other patients disappeared. Two of them dead. I didn't know what else to write, so I just lay back thinking.

Madillo never lets me do that for long. "Hey, Bul-Boo, what are you doing just lying there?" she said.

"Thinking."

Bad answer. I should have known better.

"About what?"

"Things."

"Stop being irritating, Bul-Boo, just tell me. I won't stop asking. You know that."

I did know that.

"Ten of Mum's patients have disappeared," I explained. "She's really upset about it. There must be something odd going on, because they're the very first patients who started with her at the clinic – and two of them are dead. Fred's Aunt Kiki is one of the ones who's missing. They just stopped coming to the clinic and now even their families don't know where they are."

Madillo sat up. "Disappeared? Into thin air? That's terrible. I bet it's a wizard. A wizard who has been watching the clinic, looking for victims to experiment on."

"Oh, Madillo," I said, already regretting telling her. "Please."

"We'll have to do something," she said, ignoring me. "He's probably lining up his next victims, they could be

27

anyone." She paused for a moment, suddenly realizing what I'd said. "Did you say Aunt Kiki?"

"Yes."

"Oh no, poor Fred. We have to find her quickly, before…"

"Before nothing," I said firmly. "There is no wizard. All we need to do is apply logic to this situation." I had clearly forgotten who I was talking to.

I turned on the laptop and shut the bedroom door. We have a stuffed sausage dog that we sometimes put across the bottom of the door to hide the light in case anyone checks, but I knew we wouldn't need it tonight. Mum had other things on her mind.

I opened Gmail.

I knew Mum would email that list of names to Dad straight away. She would already have them in her head and wouldn't need to wait until she was back in the office. I also knew that Dad wouldn't look at them tonight, because he always works on the theory that if he seems calm it will make Mum calm as well. (He's wrong about that, because she always knows when he's pretending to be calm.) Dad uses the same password for everything and I happen to know what it is, so I went into his account and, sure enough, there was the email from Mum. I wrote down the list in my note-book and remembered to mark the email "unread" so

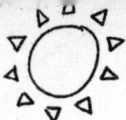

he wouldn't know I'd been in there. Easy.

Before going offline, I Googled each of the ten names. All that came up were a few Facebook accounts. Sonkwe Banda, who was now dead, was still up there. Madillo, looking over my shoulder, said, "Who's he? He's gorgeous." It was true. He had a beautiful smile. Not the smile of a person who you could imagine being dead. When I told Madillo who he was she went back to bed and covered her head with her sheet.

Having got nowhere with the names, I had to think of something else I could search for to get the investigation started. Nobody else was going to take a sensible approach to this. Certainly not Madillo.

I typed in "abductees Lusaka". Only articles about aliens and Somali pirates came up. So I tried "missing persons Zambia" and then "AIDS survivors Lusaka". Dad's agency and Mum's clinic came up. Others too. Then something on the government's AIDS programme. Plus lots of statistics on all the people in the world who are dying of the disease. And some good stuff on all the people who are actually alive and well with the disease.

But nothing that would help me.

Then, right at the very end of the second page of results there was a link that said: <u>Professor Ratsberg and Doctor Wrath promise hope.</u> I went to the site and saw

two shiny smiling men in white coats welcoming me to what they called their Holistic Healing Hope site. They looked American, anyway: in most pictures of Americans, they're smiling with their mouths wide open so you can see all their big white teeth. But maybe that's just in the ads; they're probably not all like that. There must be a few who have crooked teeth. Their tagline said, *Bringing hope and holistic healing to New York and the world*.

Dad has a thing about the word "holistic". He says it's used by people who don't know what else to say, and that when you add the word "holistic" to the word "healing" it is pure gobbledygook. Things like this irritate him. Mum says the word just means that when someone's sick you have to think about the whole body, not just one little bit of it. But Dad says that's what medicine does anyway, so why do people have to put on such pious faces when they say the word. He has a point there.

Anyway, I was getting tired, so I saved Professor Ratsberg and Dr Wrath to my favourites and turned off the computer.

It was hard to sleep that night. All I could think of was how Sonkwe would never be able to smile again, and how we would have to think of a way to tell Fred that his Aunt Kiki had disappeared.

BUL-BOO

The Menshi Curse

A Fred-less school day is always more boring than a Fred-full one, even though it was only one day. It's probably because of his jokes, even the really stupid ones.

At school it's mainly me and Madillo, Fred and, most of the time, Winifred. Sometimes she spends time with other people, but the rest of us never do. Mum says it's bad for us, because if Fred or Winifred left the school, then what would happen? But they won't, so I'm not worried about that – and we are sort of friends with the others in our class, so I think it's all right.

Madillo said to me on Sunday that she thinks Fred has a crush on me. She had a Madillo face on when she told me, a sort of half embarrassed, half laughing face.

Then she yawned, trying to pretend that she was really just bored of the whole thing.

I don't know if that's true, maybe it is, but it's weird to think about. It's also funny, because sometimes Fred can't tell the difference between us, so he must get a bit muddled if he has a crush only on me.

Madillo said that if he does *like* like me and if we start going out then we're not allowed to break up, ever. She said if we did then none of us could be friends any more, because Fred and I would hate each other and it would be all my fault that she'd lost her best friend. I don't think I could ever hate Fred and I have no intention of going out with anyone, so I told her not to worry.

We had decided to go and see him on the way home to tell him about Aunt Kiki. He only lives next door to us, on Twin Palms Road, so it was hardly out of our way.

"Fred will be very upset by the news about Aunt Kiki, so we need to be careful how we say it," I warned Madillo.

"How do you say something like that carefully?" Madillo said. *"Don't worry, Fred, but we think your aunt has been cursed by a wizard?"*

"The way we say it carefully is that I say it, not you," I said firmly.

Madillo went quiet for a while after that and I thought perhaps it was me who had silenced her. But in

fact when I looked at her it was just that she had picked up a *tsongololo* and was stroking it. As if a creature with a hundred legs and a hard shiny body actually likes being stroked a few feet above its usual habitat.

Before we reached his gate Madillo warned me that Fred had pretended to be sick this morning so we should look really worried about him when we arrived. He had texted Madillo to tell her that his mum didn't believe him, so we had to have our sad faces ready.

It would be quite hard to tell what his mum believes or doesn't believe, because she says so little. The only time I really hear her talking is when she speaks to her plants. Perhaps she doesn't have much left to say to humans.

Today she spoke to us because she had to.

"You're looking for Fred?"

As if we would ever be looking for anyone else. Like Joseph, Fred's strange little brother, or Nokokulu, his great-granny, who, according to Fred, is the most powerful witch in the whole of Zambia. Or his dad, who laughs so loudly it makes people and things jump.

"Yes, Mrs Mwamba," I said politely. I knew she wouldn't want a long conversation with me, so I kept my reply short.

"Fred's in bed," she told us, waving her hand up the stairs and turning to go outside. Fred says the only time she spends inside is when there is thunder and lightning

or when she has to go to bed. Most of the time they even eat outside on a table his dad built in their courtyard. She's very scared of lightning because she didn't grow up here, she came from England and even though they have storms there they're not like here.

When we got upstairs to his bedroom Fred was lying absolutely still with his pillow over his head.

"If you didn't know I was here, would you be able to see me?" he said from under the pillow.

"Of course we would," I said. "There's a very long Fred shape under the sheet."

He sat up. "That's a pity. I was practising collapsing my skeleton. You know, like mice do. When I get it right I might even be able to slip under locked doors or between cracks in the floorboards. Then it will be my second gift."

He frowned as he said that, as if he'd suddenly remembered why he was in bed in the first place.

"I don't think it would be particularly fair if you ended up with two gifts and I still had none," Madillo said. "And anyway, if you collapse your skeleton what are you going to do with your head?"

It's often like this – the two of them talking about something that doesn't even exist as if it does. I decided to intervene.

"If you were going to collapse your skeleton enough

to be able to slip under doors, you'd have to be rolled over by a steamroller a few times, back and forwards, so everything was squashed. Then you wouldn't be slipping under anything. You'd just be flat and dead."

"Oh, I almost forgot," said Madillo, on cue and about as carefully as an elephant in a vegetable garden. "We have news. We think Aunt Kiki has been abducted. Or worse. Most probably by a wizard."

Fred's face fell. We all knew how Aunt Kiki got very sick a few years ago. She had AIDS but she never told anyone, and because she doesn't live in Lusaka, her brother (Fred's dad) didn't notice her getting thinner and thinner. Mum said that Aunt Kiki didn't tell anyone because sometimes people are embarrassed and they think other people will look at them strangely.

That's just horrible. If a person is sick, how could you even think of looking at them strangely? It's just a disease, and now, because of all the medicine, people can live almost for ever with it if they get treated. Like they can with asthma or diabetes. No one looks strangely at someone with asthma.

Once Fred's dad discovered how sick his sister was, he persuaded her to go to the clinic Mum works at. It only took a little while on the medication for her to start putting on weight and looking like herself again. Mum says she's a real star, because now she's better she

helps in the clinic, telling the other patients why they shouldn't feel shy.

I'd thought that from then on she was going to be just fine.

Until last night.

Now, too late, Madillo remembered we were supposed to be tactful. She thought she'd pretend she hadn't said anything, so she returned to the skeleton-collapsing conversation as if she had been in it all along.

"Well, as Sister Leonisa says, anything is possible, so why not collapsing your skeleton? You just have to want it enough and it'll happen."

Fred just stared at her. "Aunt Kiki has disappeared?" he said very quietly. "She's been abducted?"

Before Madillo could answer, I jumped in. "I heard Mum saying that some of her patients have stopped coming to the clinic and Aunt Kiki is one of them. Has she said anything about it?"

He screwed his face up. "I don't know. I haven't seen her for a while. Maybe she's gone on holiday somewhere."

Poor Fred, he looked so sad.

"So," Madillo interrupted, "has anything bad happened yet? You know, with your doom thing?"

He shrugged his shoulders. "Apart from this news, no. But it's still early. And mum is sending Nokokulu

up to give me one of her potions," he added. "My own mum! She wouldn't drink one herself, so I don't see how she can let Nokokulu force one on me. I bet it's what killed Hamster."

I think he was happy the subject had been changed. He got off the bed and went down on his hands and knees to pull something out from under the bed. He held it up.

It was a poster with big black letters at the top saying: WANTED – BUT NOT BY ME. Just under that was a photograph of Nokokulu, and Fred had stuck a picture of a dead hamster on her head. Madillo started roaring with laughter and so did I. But Fred didn't seem to find it funny.

"She killed Hamster – that's why I made this. She cursed him. She told me that she'd never liked him because his eyes were too close together and that meant he couldn't be trusted. I don't understand what she was talking about. He had eyes on each side of his head – if they'd been any further apart, they'd have ended up on his ears. I'd like to see her standing up in court and saying, *'I killed him because he was not to be trusted.'* As if that's any kind of defence."

"I've never heard of a dishonest hamster," Madillo agreed, "or any kind of dishonest animal in fact. Except a human."

"You don't have proof she killed him, Fred," I said. "I thought he drowned?"

The real reason all Fred's hamsters die is that he tries to teach them to swim. I have told him they're not aquatic but he doesn't listen. I hope his new goldfish survive a little longer.

Apparently Nokokulu suggested he got a rat instead, and offered to train it to obey his every command. Nokokulu lives just behind Fred's house in a small house with a tall bed in it. She has a troupe of rats in the backyard, which all obey her, she says. And are much cleverer than hamsters. Which is true. But I'd have to agree with Fred that you wouldn't want a rat trained by Nokokulu. It could be unpredictable.

"You see," he said patiently, as if we were idiots, "she didn't kill him with her bare hands. She put a curse on him. The *Menshi* Curse. It made him believe he had to go into the water – and it was there that he died a horrible watery death."

Menshi means water in Bemba, but I think Fred just made up the name of the curse so we'd believe him. I clearly remember him once telling us how he had taught Hamster to swim. Very unsuccessfully as it turns out.

"Did she get mad when she saw the poster?" Madillo said.

"She didn't get mad in her normal way," said Fred.

"She started laughing, and she laughed so loudly and for such a long time that I got quite scared and thought she was having a fit or a heart attack or something. But she was all right. She didn't say anything about the poster after that. The worst part was that I couldn't stop laughing myself, because when you hear her laugh like that it's catching. So there I was, laughing with the chief murder suspect. Hamster would have been very upset, but he was dead so he couldn't really hear me."

There was a pause in the conversation. I looked at the two of them. Avoiding the subject was just going on for too long.

"Did you actually hear what Madillo said, Fred?" I said kindly. "Aunt Kiki is missing. We have to find her."

Before he could answer we heard Nokokulu coming up the stairs. You always know it's her because she wears really heavy boots. It doesn't matter how hot it is. I asked Fred once if he'd ever actually seen her feet and he said no. Fred always adds a small exaggeration to everything, he can't help it. So instead of just leaving it at that, he added, "Actually I believe she has hooves. That's why she wears those boots, so none of us can see them."

Madillo jumped up when she heard Nokokulu approaching. "Abducted by a wizard *or a witch*," she whispered. "But we have to go now, Fred."

Madillo has this fear/admiration thing going on with

Nokokulu. She likes the idea of her being a witch but always thinks she's about to turn her into a chameleon or a cockroach or something. Also, whenever Madillo sees Nokokulu, she bows to her. Even Nokokulu thinks that's weird. I once asked Madillo if she thought that would save her from a terrible spell being cast on her, and she said no, it was because you should never look a witch in the eye. If you do, you could be sucked into their powerful web.

I told her that in fact it's *animals* you shouldn't look in the eye when you first meet them, because they feel you are challenging them and they may attack. Dogs are like that. So are gorillas and baboons. But that fact didn't stop her bowing.

"Don't go," Fred said. His voice sometimes goes from deep back to squeaky when he's worried. "Please?"

How could we leave after that?

Madillo moved to a chair under Fred's windowsill, as far as she could get from the doorway that Nokokulu was about to walk through. I sat where I was, on the edge of Fred's bed. Fred had flopped back onto his pillow and was looking as ill as he could manage.

The door opened and Nokokulu walked in. She looked at the three of us and shook her head.

"No good this, no good at all. My great-grandchild sick in bed, dying perhaps, and you two same-same girls

come here looking for germs. No, we can't have that."

Nokokulu uses "we" when she means "I". Mum does a similar thing, except she uses "we" instead of "you". So when she says, "We really should try and keep this house tidier," she means us.

"Are you listening to me, you twins?" Nokokulu said. "Am I not right? You have a house next door that has no germs in it. A house full of doctors. It's time for you to go there and leave poor Chiti with his Nokokulu so he can get better."

She calls him Chiti even though that's his second name. It was Nokokulu who gave him that name when he was born, because she says Fred is a name better suited to a pet fish.

We didn't need a second invitation. We left quickly, avoiding Fred's eyes. We would have liked to stay and help him, but even though I don't believe the whole witch thing, Nokokulu can be a bit scary. Mainly because you never know what she's going to say to you.

"Come on," I whispered to Madillo as we walked down the stairs. "I need to go home to continue my investigation."

"What?" asked Madillo when we were back safely on our side of the hedge. "What other investigating do you need to do? We already have the culprit. It's Nokokulu. Are you blind? Why else would she have

barged into the room just as you were mentioning Aunt Kiki, who coincidentally just happens to be her granddaughter? She's probably killed all of them. You could see that's what Fred thinks too."

"Fred didn't say anything at all about it. You don't conduct investigations by jumping to ridiculous conclusions. You examine the facts and you ask the questions. You investigate."

"You know full well that she heard you, Bul-Boo. So why wasn't she upset? Why didn't she ask us anything about it? I'll tell you why – because she doesn't need to. She already knows. You *know* that she heard."

I had to admit, that part was a puzzle. Although not enough of a puzzle that we should jump to a ridiculous conclusion. There was no doubt Nokokulu had heard. Fred's dad says she has 20/20 hearing. Which, by his definition, means that she hears what she wants to hear from twenty miles away, but miraculously can't hear the things she'd rather not hear – even if they're shouted into her ear – from twenty millimetres away.

But I had other things on my mind. Something was bothering me about my search results. Why had the guys with their clinic in New York come into the results when I had definitely included Zambia in my search string?

When Mum got home I asked her innocently, "Have you ever heard of men called Ratsberg and

Wrath from New York? Do they have some connection with Zambia?"

"*Ratbag*, you mean?" Mum said in disgust. She's not very good at hiding her feelings. "No, thankfully, neither of those *genocidaires* has anything to do with Zambia. They did enough damage in South Africa for ten lifetimes. Why do you ask?"

"Oh, just a school project," I said quickly. "It's nothing."

"A school project on what? Don't tell me Sister Leonisa has put you onto them? It'd be the kind of rubbish she'd believe in. God Almighty, what goes on in that school?"

I should have known not to raise it. I'd just thought that in her current mood she might not have the energy to ask me why I wanted to know. I should have known better.

"We were doing stuff about orphans and their names came up. I just thought they sounded funny."

"Funny, all right. Funny *evil*," she said under her breath, stirring the pot of soup as if it was the enemy.

"Anyway, I'll just go and finish my homework now," I said, trying to adopt Madillo's breezy tone.

She didn't answer, just carried on stirring like a crazy woman. Now I had a new word to look up: *genocidaires*. It sounded like "genocide", so I supposed it had

something to do with mass murder and war. Not that that really helped, because if they were in New York, I would not really put them on a list of suspects.

I thought I should have a list, though, and even though I was most definitely not ready to put Nokokulu on it, I did scribble "N" down, in pencil. It was a start.

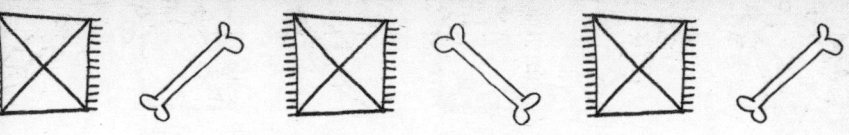

FRED

Nokokulu and the Man-Beast

My Great-granny Nokokulu is an unusual person. To put it mildly. She is full of powers. They're all stuck in a spindly skinny body that creaks around the place like a rusty bicycle. She complains that soon she'll die and there'll be no real witch left in our family.

She is wrong about that. First of all, of course, she is never going to die. There is no hope of that at all. Secondly, certain other people in this family have powers. And she knows that. That is why she is always trying to teach me the values she thinks I'm losing.

"Chiti," she says, "what's the point of sitting in front of a screen where little idiot characters run around shooting each other? One day you'll forget what real people look like, then what? Silly little voices, chirping

and squawking like chickens with sore throats. That's not life. I'll show you what life is really about, then you'll forget all these computer things."

She calls me Chiti rather than Fred. It's my middle name and nobody else uses it. Today, after the twins had left (and after she'd given me her medicine, which might have made me feel better if I'd been sick in the first place), she sat down on my bed and made an announcement.

"You and I – the Great Nokokulu and her great-grandson Chiti, named after the most powerful chief in the whole of Zambia – are going on a journey. You are growing big now, and I can see that you may have some of my powers running through your body. Not as many as I have, nobody has that many, but a few. They'll do for the moment."

"We're going on a journey?" I said, my voice giving that irritating squeak it seems to have all the time now. "I can't go anywhere. I'm sick."

It wasn't really much good telling her that, because she never listens. But it was worth a try.

"I'll plan carefully, and then we'll go," she said. "You and I, to the place where the Man-Beast has returned. The Man-Beast who thinks his powers will protect him. He is wrong. He has been sleeping for too many years – his memory has left him. A beast with a bad

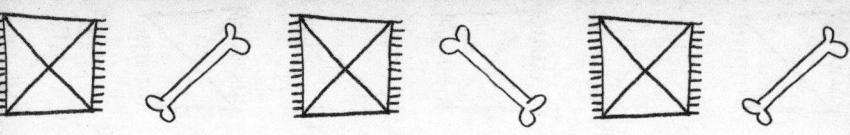

memory is no beast at all. You will come with me, and watch. And learn."

She looked at me. I was probably looking confused, because that's exactly how I felt. What was a Man-Beast with a bad memory?

"Ah, Chiti. You won't remember, your mind is also like a big sieve, but your grandmother was taken from us. Before you were even born. On the day your father and Kiki came into this world."

I sat up, forgetting I was supposed to be weak. "Aunt Kiki and Dad are twins? No one ever told me that."

"Twins, brother and sister, what's the difference?" she said, waving her hand around. "The point is, this creature has to be stopped before he kills again. Once every forty years he comes, before the rainy season. Now is his time. So, you and I will go. Just us alone. Not your father. Not your mother. And most certainly not the *mpundu* from next door." She says *mpundu* as if it's a dirty word, when all it means is "twins". "It is you who must come with me, because it is only you who will understand, only you who will not fear him."

Even the word "Man-Beast" was terrifying, so I wasn't sure why she thought I wouldn't be afraid of it, whatever or whoever it was. Looking on the bright side, at least she'd admitted out loud that I possess magical powers. If I went on this trip, perhaps it would move

me up the rankings of People with Special Powers and Bul-Boo would finally believe me.

But maybe not.

Maybe I should have just listened to Bul-Boo's voice in my head saying, "Stop being a twit for one minute and use your brain." And my brain was telling me loud and clear that this trip was going to be bad news. Whatever Nokokulu had in mind, it would be something that only she understood and it was ninety-nine per cent likely to be bad.

"But, Nokokulu," I said, "I'm so sick that my stomach feels like it's caught between the jaws of a giant crocodile. So sick that I don't know if I would even make it as far as the car."

I closed my eyes to make her believe that I didn't even have enough strength to keep them open. And of course I hoped I could make her disappear, that she would be gone in a puff of smoke when I opened them again, but I doubted I had that much power yet.

"Sick you may be, or not, but we are going," she said, unfortunately still there. "To Ng'ombe Ilede where the bones of my ancient forebears lie. This trip will finally make you, the inheritor of my powers, into a good and proper member of this great family."

"But if I die while we're travelling in your car, what will Mum and Dad say?" I asked her. "And anyway, it's

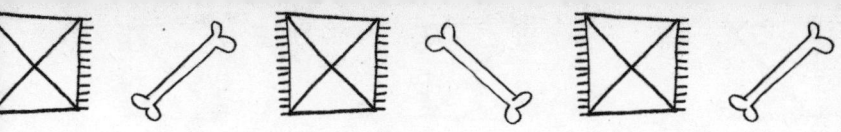

the Tonga-speaking people who are from Ng'ombe Ilede, not our ancestors."

"Be quiet if you have nothing sensible to say," she said. "Our ancestors travelled far and wide. They were like me. Powerful. Not for them one village for life. All of Zambia was their kingdom. We will leave on Saturday morning after the sun has risen high into the sky."

"I have schoolwork and I've got things arranged with Bul-Boo and Madillo," I said, trying to sound decisive. "I can't go. Sorry about that."

"Lying again, Chiti? I don't mind that. All children tell lies. As long as they are not big lies that sit in your stomach and eat away at your body until there is nothing left but a pile of bones. But you know there is no point trying your lies on me, big or small. I always know."

She stood looking at me and I suddenly remembered what Bul-Boo had said about Aunt Kiki.

"Nokokulu, you know you were talking about Aunt Kiki? When is she coming to visit us again?" I asked.

"Why, all of a sudden, do you want to know about Aunt Kiki?" she said, raising her voice. "You leave her alone. Don't be asking me."

With that she turned and stomped out of the room, banging the door behind her.

Perhaps the twins were right. Perhaps something

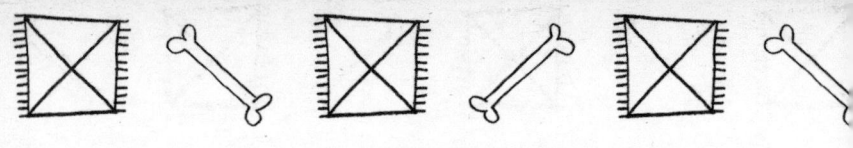

terrible had happened to Aunt Kiki and they weren't telling me. And now I was being forced to go on some trip to who knows where. Everything was going wrong. My Prophecies of Doom are always right, and this one was only heading in one direction. Aunt Kiki, even when she was really sick, has always been the kindest person I know.

My only hope was that my parents would for once stand up to her and refuse to let me go on this suicide mission. That hope faded fast. She met Mum in the garden and announced her plan. I could hear because I have 20/20 hearing, just like her. Also, in this particular instance my window was open and Mum was just outside it, by the rose bushes.

"Chiti is coming with me for a little picnic on Saturday," Nokokulu announced. If she ever, by mistake, calls me Fred, she certainly never does it in front of Mum. According to her it was all Mum's fault that we got the names Fred and Joseph, and Dad was soft in the head to have allowed it. Joseph's second name is Chola, but Nokokulu just calls him "boy". (She calls me that sometimes as well.) None of his names suit him, she says. Imagine if we were all like her and called people whatever name we thought suited them? She'd be called a few things she wouldn't like, I can tell you that.

"Did you ask Chiti?" Mum said.

"Ha! All this asking. He's a small boy. He doesn't get asked – he gets told."

"You know, Nokokulu," Mum said, almost whispering, "you shouldn't be so bossy with the boys. If you were less bossy, maybe they'd like you a bit more."

It was as if, after all these years, Mum still didn't know who she was dealing with.

"Bossy? What kind of a word is that? We don't have that word in ChiBemba, especially not for great-grandmothers talking to their great-grandchildren. Small children need to listen. If they don't listen, they won't learn. What is the use of me being on this earth for nearly one hundred years then not passing on what I have learnt to the ones that follow in my footsteps? Maybe where you come from things are different. Yes, they are of my blood, but this doesn't mean I must spoil them. No, no, no. Not me. I'm different from you English."

"We each have our own ways," said Mum, in her giving-up voice.

"And our own ways are not always good. Look at my own precious girl: she thought she was too big to listen. Look what happened to her."

Nokokulu was going on about my grandmother again. Although it's funny to think of her as a grandmother when she was only sixteen when she died.

"I understand, Nokokulu." Mum had not only given up but was now feeling sorry for her. "It's very sad. You're right."

Right, Mum? About what? About a woman who's been dead for ever or about telling us what to do whether we like it or not?

Sometimes I despair of my mum.

"You have strong hands for the garden, Sarah," said the witch, changing the subject very successfully. That was as close to a kind word as she was ever going to give my mother.

"Thank you," said Mum.

"Maybe," continued Nokokulu, never wanting to finish on a good note in case somebody might start thinking well of her, "maybe when you are older you will get sense and instead of planting useless bushes and flowers you will start growing vegetables."

BUL-BOO

The Baobab That Fell Over

After Sister had told us the story about Bukoko the Little Tick Child I looked up Ng'ombe Ilede. Sister was right about one thing: it is also called The Place of the Sleeping Cow or The Place of the Cow Who Lies Down, because of a baobab tree that fell over but carried on growing. In some ways it does look like a sleeping cow (no one has decided yet whether this is a normal cow or an elephant cow) but in other ways it looks like a strange human trying to do sit-ups.

I suppose Sister was also right about another thing: it is an ancient burial ground, so the pretend body of Bukoko the Little Tick Child *could* have been buried there, if she had ever existed. But I still think Sister made that part up for dramatic effect.

While I was looking it up, Madillo came in. Well, she didn't just come in, she bounced in like a rubber ball.

"Fred just sent you a message," she said, holding up my phone. Nokokulu is taking him, this Saturday, to Ng'ombe Ilede. Can you believe that? I sometimes wonder if she and Sister Leonisa are in cahoots, or maybe they exist on the same astral plane."

She showed me the text, oblivious firstly to the fact that the phone is actually mine and she shouldn't be reading my messages, and secondly to the fact that there is no such thing as an astral plane.

"Coincidence. That's all. They happen all the time," I said to her. "And he's pretty lucky to be going to a place of such significant archaeological interest." I had just read that on the Wikipedia page and it sounded pretty good. But Madillo didn't seem too impressed.

"Coincidence? I don't think so. On exactly the same day that Sister tells us that particular story, and Nokokulu hears us talking about her abducting people, she announces that she wants Fred to come with her on a little drive. To an ancient burial ground! That's more than a coincidence, that's creepy. Why would you take your great-grandson on a trip to visit graves? There's something wrong with that."

"People visit graves all over the world," I argued. "It's an interesting thing to see how old the people were

who died, and when they died." I was trying not to wonder about the coincidence.

Madillo looked at the computer screen. "And, you see: Ng'ombe Ilede. Right there. On the computer. How weird is that?"

"Not one bit weird. I looked it up, as I always do when Sister tells us a new story. Mainly to find out how much of it is true."

Madillo shook her head. "No. If you add in the fact that Fred had one of his premonitions this morning, this is not looking good, Bul-Boo, not good at all."

My phone beeped and Madillo looked at the message.

"Fred wants us to come to the hedge to talk about it," she said. "Let's go."

When Madillo is a little bit scared about something she gets excited at the same time. Maybe both those things happen in the same part of the brain. Dad showed me these pictures in *New Scientist* once where they took scans of the brains of people eating chocolate. When they ate the first bits of chocolate the happiness part of the brain lit up on the scans. Which makes sense. But as they ate more and more, other parts lit up, the parts that were trying to tell them to stop. Which also makes sense. I suppose you can get sick of too much chocolate, although in our house we never get the opportunity to try that theory out.

I must remember to put into my black notebook this fact: The happiness part of Madillo's brain lights up just a little bit when she's scared.

BUL-BOO

Roaming Ancestors and Sacrifices

When we got down to the gap in the hedge between our houses Fred was waiting for us.

"Now do you believe me when I tell you about my premonitions?" he asked me.

I didn't answer, mainly because I didn't want to upset him by saying no.

"I don't want to go with her on my own. We're leaving on Saturday morning at eight o'clock and she's planning to go for the whole day," he said, looking worried. When Fred looks worried you feel really sorry for him. It's something about the way he wrinkles up his forehead.

"Can't you tell your mum and dad that?" Madillo asked.

"I did, but Dad said it would be interesting and that it's always good to know where you come from, even though I don't come from there."

"Don't your dad and Nokokulu come from the Northern Province, when Ng'ombe Ilede is in the Southern?" I said.

"Yes, but try telling Nokokulu that. She just rubs her hands together and tells me that her ancestors roamed all over the country. She says she wants me to become a proper member of this 'great family'. Whatever that means."

"A proper member? Does she mean traditionally or what?" Madillo said.

"It could mean anything, but I don't want to be part of some kind of ceremony," Fred added with a shudder.

I like the word "shudder". It sounds like the thing it's describing.

"Ceremony? Like a sacrifice?" Madillo said, jumping over every possible reasonable explanation straight to the worst one.

"Nokokulu is not about to sacrifice anything," I said, "least of all her favourite great-grandson. Maybe she just wants to teach Fred some manners. She's always going on about manners."

"You're forgetting the main thing, Bul-Boo," Madillo said. "You always forget the main thing. She's a

witch. And witches sacrifice things to appease the gods. You name any country in the world and you'll find human sacrifice. Look at the Germans, and the Tibetans and the Celts and the Aztecs and—"

"Do the Germans sacrifice people?" Fred asked, temporarily distracted from his own fate.

"Well, not so much today, but they did. Don't you remember Sister Leonisa telling us about the Windeby Boy? He was German and the same age as you, Fred—"

"Fred wasn't there for the Human Sacrifice lessons," I interrupted her. "It was when you went with your mum to England, Fred, and missed two weeks of school. The Windeby Boy was one of the ones they found in a bog in Germany."

"And he had a headband on and long blond hair. Not like yours, Fred," Madillo added, to try to make up for telling Fred that the boy had been the same age as him.

"Madillo," I said, before she could continue, "Nokokulu is *not* going to sacrifice Fred. That's just ridiculous." I was glad that Fred had missed those lessons. They had been very gruesome and he'd have felt even worse now if he'd sat through them.

"Well, what if she wants to experiment on him with her curses and spells? What if she decides to change him into a chameleon just because she can?" Madillo said.

"I've never seen her change a human into anything," Fred said, shaking his head. "I know she's a witch and everything, but she wouldn't do that."

At last one of them was seeing just a little sense.

"I don't know if I should tell you this," he continued, his expression changing, "but she was also talking about something she called the Man-Beast, some terrible creature with a bad memory. She was speaking almost as if we're going there to hunt him down."

Now I could see his worry turning into real fear.

"She's mad," I said. "Man-Beast? There's no such thing."

"She thinks he's the one who took away my granny. She says he appears every forty years and now he's come to Ng'ombe Ilede."

"That's it!" Madillo said, bowing her head in the same way she does to Nokokulu. "It's him – the Man-Beast. *He's* the one taking all Mum's patients. He's the one who has Aunt Kiki. I was wrong. It's not Nokokulu; it's him. The Man-Beast has returned and is rampaging about the land stealing people. Who knows who'll be next?" She peered round the hedge as she spoke, as if to make sure he wasn't standing there listening while he decided which one of us to take.

Way to go, Madillo. Why don't you make things ten times as bad?

Madillo leant forward and grabbed hold of Fred's hand. "We won't abandon you, Fred. We won't let the Man-Beast claim you as his next victim."

"Stop it!" I said. "Stop it now! There's no such thing. Nokokulu is the biggest liar I've ever met. She's just trying to frighten you, Fred. And you, Madillo, think for a minute. Have you ever seen a Man-Beast, whatever on earth that might be?"

Madillo looked a little deflated but it wasn't enough to stop her.

"Just because you haven't seen something doesn't mean it doesn't exist," she said. "And, if you remember, Bukoko's mother said Bukoko was killed by a *two-legged* hyena in exactly the same place."

Fred nodded. "True," he said. "Very true. And that explains how my granny disappeared."

Suddenly everyone believed Sister Leonisa's story because it suited their argument, even Fred, in spite of the fact that he hadn't been there to hear it!

"You're both forgetting the main point," I said. "This is real life. Aunt Kiki and seven other people, who all go to Mum's clinic, have disappeared. They can't have been eaten by a monster otherwise the two who have already died would have had bite marks on them. And, if you remember, Bukoko's mother made up the story about the two-legged hyena because she

was embarrassed. *And*" – it had to be said – "we have yet to eliminate your great-granny from our enquiries, Fred."

I didn't mention that she was only on the list in pencil and as an initial. I just wanted to get their attention.

"Yes, of course," said Madillo, pleased I was even considering Nokokulu as a suspect.

Fred was silent. He looked down at the ground, which is what he does when he doesn't want to answer a question. I've never understood that, as if the ground will somehow save him.

"Two died?" he said finally, in a small voice. "I didn't know that. I saw Aunt Kiki a few weeks ago. They would have told me if something had happened to her."

I was almost as bad as Madillo, blurting out hurtful things without thinking.

"Sorry, Fred, I forgot we hadn't told you everything. We don't have a lot of facts, but I overheard Mum telling Dad that your Aunt Kiki and seven others who used to come to the clinic have all disappeared. Perhaps," I said, "Nokokulu hasn't been told yet. Maybe she didn't hear the news?"

"Oh, she heard. Definitely. 20/20, you know," said Fred.

"That's it then," said Madillo. "She probably has them all locked away somewhere. She's probably

sacrificing them to the ancestors one by one in order to get her daughter back, the one she's always talking about."

"Including her granddaughter Kiki?" I said, trying to sound rational. "Come on now. What do you think, Fred?"

"I don't know," said Fred. "I asked her about Aunt Kiki. I asked when she was coming to visit."

Fred is a master of letting information out in dribs and drabs.

"And?" I said, trying not to sound impatient.

"She shouted at me and then stomped out of the room. She didn't answer my question, she just looked really, really angry."

I looked at Madillo. She raised her eyebrows. "What did I tell you?" was all she said.

"Do you want us to come with you to Ng'ombe Ilede?" I asked Fred, a part of me hoping that he'd say no.

"Yes," he said gratefully. "Yes, yes, yes."

My hope faded as quickly as it had arrived. But he said, "Nokokulu specifically said you can't come."

"Both of us?" Madillo asked.

Fred nodded.

I carried on regardless. "We'll have to persuade Mum and Dad – they've warned us never to get into the car

with her. Nothing to do with her being a murderous witch: Dad says she's just not to be trusted on the road."

Nokokulu has this bright yellow car that looks about as old as she is. Fred says it's lucky it's bright yellow because at least other drivers can see her coming and get off the road fast. She has a pile of cushions on the driver's seat so she can see over the steering wheel, and on the dashboard she has a stuffed rat. A real one – she says it's to make sure thieves don't steal the car. Its mouth is wide open so you can see all of its small pointy teeth. Fred says she stuffed it herself after cursing it to death. He's just relieved it isn't a hamster.

Fred looked as if he was deciding whether to defend her or not. She is his great-grandmother, after all, and you are kind of obliged to defend your family, even when you don't always feel like it – and even if they could very well be a homicidal maniac.

"Well, Dad says she's not that bad," he said at last. "She just drives very slowly. And she's never had an accident, apart from that one man on his bicycle who got in her way. He was all right afterwards, just a few bruises. His bicycle was a bit mangled but Dad bought him a new one. And that was before she got the cushions, so she couldn't see the road properly – or cyclists."

"Well," Madillo said, "I still don't think Mum and Dad will let us go, and if Nokokulu doesn't want us …

we'll just have to sneak into the car."

"How?" I asked. "How does anyone sneak past Nokokulu? Or Mum for that matter?" I excluded Dad because we all know how to sneak past him.

"We'll tell them we're going for a sleepover at Fred's and then just before you leave we'll get into the boot," Madillo said, as if she'd done this a hundred times before. "And we'll be back in the afternoon anyway, so they won't even know we've left."

"I suppose *technically* we'll be telling the truth," I said, "because we will be staying at your house for the night. We just won't tell them the other bit. And we will be back in the afternoon, won't we, Fred?"

"We should be," said Fred. "Ng'ombe Ilede is only about two hours' drive away, just past Siavonga."

"We'll have to tell your mum and dad that we'll be going back home before you leave," I said quietly. "Otherwise they'll wonder where we are. Will they be up to help you get ready in the morning?"

Fred shook his head mournfully. He does mournful better than anyone I know. Sometimes he imagines that his parents neglect him terribly. Which they don't.

"OK, so we'll say goodbye as if we're going home early in the morning, then we'll sneak into the car and you'll have to close the boot before she sees," Madillo said. "We'll have to bring a knife or something in case

she doesn't open the boot when you get there. Then we can release ourselves to stop us suffocating or dying of overheating. I'd hate to die of overheating."

When Madillo plans things she always takes into account every eventuality. I was waiting for the rest of the list. Sure enough...

"We'll put water bottles into the boot and food supplies – chocolate probably, like the mountaineers. Or is that only so the St Bernards can find them?"

"Chocolate has nothing to do with dogs, Madillo," I said. "In fact if you feed a dog chocolate it can die. St Bernards carry brandy to lost mountaineers to warm them up, they don't sniff out chocolate bars. Plus we can scrap the knife. Nothing could suffocate in Nokokulu's car – have you seen how many holes there are in the bodywork?"

"Anyway, we should probably also put pillows in the boot so we don't bump our heads and get concussion," Madillo said, ignoring me.

At this rate we were setting ourselves up for a few months in the boot of the car.

"Are you sure?" Fred said.

We both looked at him. Sometimes we forget that someone else is there, even when that person is the main subject of the conversation. Mum says it's because we hear each other more easily than we hear anyone else.

"Are we sure about what?" we said in unison.

"About coming with me?"

I thought for a minute. If we went with him it would mean having to lie about where we were, and I hate doing that to Mum and Dad because they don't do that to us.

Madillo and Fred were looking at me. Fred for his own reasons, which I don't always want to think about, and Madillo because she was waiting for me to say, "Yes, we're sure."

There are things that are important in life, and one is that you should always look after your friends. Fred is more than our best friend, he is the one person we know almost as well as we know each other. We couldn't let him go on his own, however many lies we would have to tell.

"Yes. We're sure. We'll do it," I said. "If you promise it's only a day trip and that when we get there you'll let us out. We couldn't let you go by yourself – that'd be awful."

Fred actually blushed when I said that and then I felt funny. I was waiting for Madillo to say something, but she didn't. Thank goodness.

But I am starting to think she's right about Fred having a crush on me.

Sister Leonisa says that the "sickness of love" turns

clever people into marshmallows, but that luckily she's never been affected by it. It would be hard to think of Sister in love. I can't imagine her looking at someone adoringly. Sister has only a few looks: a glare, a withering look, a pitying stare, an almost-kind look (that's reserved for Fred the Favourite), a "prove that I'm wrong" look and an "end of conversation, raised eyebrows" look. None of those, apart from the almost-kind one, would go down too well with someone she was supposed to be in love with. And the almost-kind one is a bit strange because she twists her face to get to it, as if the kind muscles are not used to moving. Which I suppose they aren't.

"Fred, you have to come in now," Joseph called from the back door.

Madillo always used to think that Fred's little brother, Joseph, was a hermaphrodite. But she doesn't any more; she told me the other day that she only thought that because she believed that a hermaphrodite was the same as an amoeba, where one cell splits into two. She couldn't believe he was Fred's brother because they are so different, so she thought he had created himself. I did explain to her that if that was the case there would be two identical Josephs and at any moment they might split into more, then there would be hundreds of them before your very eyes. I explained

how it's called binary fission, but she said that didn't sound as nice as hermaphrodite. Imagine if science was about what sounded nice!

When Fred didn't answer, Joseph ran up to the hedge. "Mum says you have to come and wash the dishes because you're better now, and the next-door twins have to go home."

He didn't look at us when he said this. He never does. Maybe he's scared of us.

"OK," Fred said, resigned. "So I'll see you in the morning on the way to school and I'll tell Mum you're coming to stay over tomorrow night?"

"OK," I said.

"We didn't even discuss what will happen when Nokokulu discovers us," Madillo said after Fred had gone. "That's going to be terrible."

"Let's talk about that tomorrow," I said. "And anyway, what can she do to us?"

I paused as the question left my lips. "On second thoughts, don't answer that."

The last thing I wanted was a list of the ways a witch can kill her victims. It would be a very *long* one.

BUL-BOO

Science, Witches and Disappearing Patients

When Mum and Dad arrive back from work in the afternoons it isn't always the best time to ask them anything, but today we had no option. Anyway it wasn't asking them a big thing, we often go to sleep over at Fred's.

They get really tired at work, Mum especially. Dad seems to be able to put things out of his mind but Mum can't. I could see Mum had been crying when she came in this evening. I hate seeing that. If Madillo ever sees her crying she thinks it's because they're going to get divorced – but it's not. It's always work things. Mum told me once that if she'd known how much sadness there was going to be in medicine she might have become a beautician. At least then all her

customers would have been happy when they left her. But I know she doesn't think that all the time. Anyway she's a bit clumsy so she'd smudge the faces of her customers if she was a beautician and they wouldn't be too happy about that.

When she's been crying it's most often about children whose parents have died.

There are a million AIDS orphans in our country. One million. I don't really like the way they are called AIDS orphans. You never hear about cancer orphans or heart-attack orphans or even malaria orphans. It makes them sound as though they are more than just orphans, as if that's not bad enough on its own. Dad says it's because people need to know how terrible this disease is. But how could anyone not know that?

It's seeing those children that upsets Mum the most – when little babies are brought into the clinic by their older brothers and sisters who have to grow up very fast and become mini parents. I heard her speaking to Dad about it once, when I was supposed to be asleep. I suppose a lot of what I learn about Mum and Dad is when I'm supposed to be asleep. This time it was a pretty serious thing.

She said she wanted to adopt another child.

Another child? Just like that. As if we're not enough for her. As if we don't need to be asked.

Dad said that it would make no difference as there are millions of children all over the world who need a home, and we couldn't adopt all of them. I didn't listen to any more because once I'd got over the shock of it, all I could hear were the words "another child". So, were we the first adopted children? It's not that I'd have minded if we were, because then we'd have two family histories. (I like family histories, I've traced ours back to my great-great-great-grandmother.) But I wished they'd told us. Luckily I knew I was related to Madillo at least.

The next day, I asked Mum and she just laughed and put a mirror in front of me and said, "Who do you look like?"

I gave her the obvious answer: Madillo. But I don't think that was what she was looking for.

"Yes, Bul-Boo, we all know that. But both of you look like half me and half Dad, so you can't be adopted. Although we have been thinking about adopting a child. How would you feel about that?"

Mum often asks us how we'd feel about something but normally it's after she's already decided that's what she's going to do. She's what Dad calls a benign dictator. She rules us with a smile on her face and mostly makes the right decisions.

"We'd feel OK, I think. I'll ask Madillo. Maybe adopt

someone the same age as Joseph so he has a friend? How does Dad feel about it?"

It's always a bit harder for her to be the benign dictator with Dad. She has to use more persuasion on him.

"He'll be fine," she said, "but we haven't decided." Translated that meant Dad was not too sure about the whole thing.

I'd like to have an extra brother or sister, I think. Or both, especially if I knew that their parents had died and they were alone in this world. When I told Madillo about it she got a glazed look on her face and said, "That means we'd be their saviours." Which was a bit extreme.

But that was quite a long time ago and we've heard nothing since then, so I suppose Mum's still trying to persuade Dad.

Anyway, I knew the reason for her tears today, and it had nothing to do with orphans.

This problem of the disappeared patients was one that I knew I could do something about. I wasn't blowing my own trumpet, as Dad would say, but I *was* the only person in this house with decent detecting skills. Seeing Mum upset just made me more certain that I had to follow the one slim lead I had to go on. We had no choice. We would have to go on this trip and study every move of Suspect Number 1. The one who shall be known as "N".

I couldn't help rushing my words a little when I told Mum and Dad that we were planning a sleepover at Fred's on Friday. Even though it was technically the truth, I still felt bad.

"And Fred's mum is OK with it?" Mum asked.

"She's fine," I said. "She doesn't really notice us much." Which is true.

Madillo, in the meantime, was just sitting at the kitchen table eating toast covered with something unidentifiable, as if she had nothing to do with any of us. She's good at that, being the invisible, innocent, toast-eating twin. That way she never has to tell a lie. But I have told her it makes no difference because she is aiding and abetting me, which just makes her a silent guilty party.

"And the witch?" Mum said.

I probably forgot to mention that Mum also thinks that Nokokulu is a witch. Mum who is a doctor – who spent years studying science to become a doctor. She thinks our neighbour Fred's great-granny is a witch. Sort of.

Dad is on my side in the Witch versus Science debate.

He didn't say anything this time, just clutched his head as if he was in agony.

Mum looked embarrassed, like Madillo does when

she's said something ridiculous. I think sometimes she lets things like that out before thinking about them.

"I was only joking," she added quickly.

She should have just kept quiet and let the whole thing pass with a mere head clutch.

"No you weren't," Dad said. "You actually think that here, on Twin Palms Road in twenty-first century Zambia, we live next door to a witch. Which part of our medical degree was taught under the heading Witches and Other Magical Things? I must have been asleep that day."

"I just think there are some things that science can't explain, that's all. It's not a sin," Mum said, leaving the room. A good way to end an argument, I suppose, leaving the other person with no one to argue with any more.

Dad looked at Madillo still munching away. "This is all your fault, you know," he said, grinning. "My wife, your dear mother, never thought anything like this till the day you came home from Fred's and announced that we now live next door to a witch. It was the day Nokokulu came to live with them, do you remember?"

Madillo nodded.

If Madillo is involved in a less than truthful occasion she just nods or mumbles. I can tell immediately. All she wanted right then was for Dad to leave the room in case

he went back to the subject of us going over to Fred's. She wasn't even defending her witch theory.

Dad shook his head. "So what are you going to do at Fred's?"

This time she couldn't keep silent as it was a direct question.

"Nothing much. Usual stuff," she replied.

Dad is very easily satisfied by answers that aren't answers, so he just said, "Oh," and left the room. Probably to hunt down Mum so he could carry on the argument.

Mum always tells him that he should listen to us with more than half an ear, which is an expression I still cannot quite picture. But in this case she was right.

If it had been Mum asking the question she would have wanted to know what "nothing much" meant and what kind of "usual stuff". But, luckily for us, not only was she embarrassed by her witch comment, but her mind was also on other things. Sad things.

BUL-BOO

Doomed Archaeologists

On the way to school today we stopped to wait for Fred at his gate and Nokokulu was in the garden. She didn't say anything, just waved at us with a maniacal grin on her face. I first discovered the word "maniacal" when I was trying to describe Sister Leonisa and Dad suggested it. I suppose it's not really fair but it does describe Sister better than any other word does.

Madillo grabbed my arm. "She knows. She knows what we're planning – you can see it."

"She always looks like that," I said. "How could she possibly know?"

"She has ways and means," Madillo said quietly, still holding onto my arm.

At that point Nokokulu said, "Ha!"

Just that, nothing more. Madillo may well have been right. Nokokulu's voice had a triumphant sound to it.

Fred came running down the driveway, his shoes in one hand and his lunch in the other. He is always late.

"Sorry, sorry, I'm ready now," he said as he waved goodbye to Nokokulu with the hand holding the shoes.

We started walking, and Madillo said, "Fred, I think she knows our plan."

"No, she doesn't," he said confidently. "If she did she would have said something. She's no good at keeping her mouth shut, you know that. Do you think she would have stayed silent when she saw you if she knew the plan? Never."

"But if she does discover it, then what?"

Fred paused. "Then I'm doomed. Totally, infinitely, inextricably and horrendously doomed."

Fred likes long words. He says they're his indelible trademark. (See what I mean?) I think that of the three of us he is probably the most dramatic. Nothing is ever just ordinary with Fred – it's always either the very, very best or the very, very worst.

"That would be your second doom prophecy day in a row," Madillo said, with a suitably stricken face.

"No, that can only happen once the doom of the first one has been fulfilled. That's how it works. Doom prophecy – doom fulfilment," Fred said.

The King and Queen of Exaggeration, that's who they are.

As an example. If there was a green mamba in the mango tree in our back garden, I would say, "There's a green mamba in the garden, we need to find Ifwafwa, the snake man, to take it away."

Madillo would say, "You will never believe what just happened. The biggest green mamba ever seen in this road, probably in this city, is in the mango tree out the back. No one knows how it came to be here, but it's very strange that it chose our back garden and our mango tree. We'll have to see whether we can track down Ifwafwa to help us solve the mystery."

And Fred would say, "A cataclysmic event has just taken place. We are all lucky to have survived it. An evil spirit, clothed in the sinuous body of a green mamba, has taken up residence in the twins' mango tree. If Ifwafwa is still alive we will summon him. If he isn't, we are all condemned to a miserable and slow death."

Yes. I am surrounded by them.

Madillo looked at Fred. "Well, if she doesn't know we'll just have to make sure it carries on that way, won't we?"

I was starting to get a small niggle of regret in the back of my mind about this plan. Here we were, about to smuggle ourselves into the boot of an ancient yellow

car being driven by an even older, slightly mad person who had, let's not forget, recently become a kidnapping and murder suspect. Not to mention the rumour of a Man-Beast on the loose.

Mum and Dad would have no idea at all where we were, and I would be losing a full day in my investigation (which in my black notebook I was now calling An Enquiry into Unusual Disappearances).

Mum once took us to watch this movie called *127 Hours* about a guy who got trapped in a canyon for 127 hours and had to cut his own arm off to escape. The main point of the movie, as far as I could see, was that you should always tell people where you're going so that if you disappear they know where to look for you. This guy didn't tell anyone, and every hour that passed while he was helplessly trapped by this rock he regretted it.

I didn't want to end up with a movie being made about us called *The Mystery of the Disappearing Twins*. Imagine if Mum and Dad had to appear on ZTV crying and saying, "They never told us where they were going. All they said was that they were sleeping over at Fred's house next door. Please bring our daughters back safely."

Maybe the newspapers would accuse them of being careless parents, which would be awful. And even more awful would be the fact that we would have just

disappeared off the face of the earth, two lying ungrateful children.

On the plus side, Dad gave us mini smart phones for our last birthday, despite Mum objecting to it, because they have GPS in them and he said it meant we could always be found. I'm not sure if that works when the battery is flat though, and Madillo's is always flat. I'll just have to make sure mine is charged.

We walked into the classroom and Sister's face twisted itself into the almost-kind look. "Ah, Fred, you're back. Are you better?"

He nodded. He's not that delighted about being Sister's favourite, but she doesn't seem to notice.

On Sister's desk there was a pile of books and pictures about Egypt. I love it when we do Egypt, but that's normally in History. Sister had never done it with us in Religious Studies before.

"Sit down, sit down," she said. "Wait quietly for the others, then we'll begin. We're going back to Ng'ombe Ilede today."

I saw Madillo looking sideways at Fred. He went a little pale I think.

As soon as everyone else was in, Sister started. She wrote A R C H A E O L O G I S T S in big uneven letters on the blackboard, and next to them she drew a skull and crossbones. Like this:

"So," she said. "Archaeologists. The scourge of the living and the dead. Men and their shovels, digging up people and things that have no wish whatsoever to be dug up. If I ever hear of one of you becoming an archaeologist I will tell the world that I had nothing to do with it."

She stood there looking accusingly at each of us in turn. If any of us did happen to become an archaeologist, I can't think that the first question we'd be asked would be "Did Sister Leonisa put you up to this?"

In my mind I was ticking the new column in the little red book: **STORIES THAT HAVE DEATH IN THEM**.

"There they are, the thousand-year-old people, sleeping away peacefully in their graves, and what happens? A nosy little man comes knocking on their coffin walls, 'Let me in, let me in, I want to take you to pieces and inspect your bones.'

"But, what you need to remember is that these nosy archaeologists have the most dangerous job in the world. Why? Because, naturally enough, the thousand-year-old people don't want to be disturbed, so they breathe

their Dead Breath all over the prying men, and one by one they all die in horrible deathly ways. Which serves them right."

I do sometimes wonder whether Sister just dresses up as a nun. I don't think nuns are supposed to say things like "serves them right" when people die. And since when has a death been anything other than deathly?

"Does every archaeologist in the whole world die like that?" Fred asked. He's allowed to ask and answer questions to his heart's content.

"Yes, Fred, every last miserable one of them. So, for your own good, don't even think of that as a job," Sister said.

"In Egypt," she continued, "which is the favourite hunting ground of the archaeologists, this has a name: the Curse of the Pharaohs. Anyone looking for scientific proof" – she didn't even need to look at me – "can find it there. Off they went, a merry band of prying men, and they dug up the tomb of a boy king Tutankhamun. One of them, Howard Carter, walked into the tomb, and the minute he did so his pet canary, who had stayed at home, was killed by a cobra. Instant yellow-bird death."

I wondered if she thought the canary deserved it too.

"That exact minute, boys and girls, that he dared enter the tomb of the famous Tutankhamun. Now," she picked up one of her pictures, "tell me what you see."

She held up a picture of a pharaoh with a big black arrow pointing to a golden cobra on his crown. Just in case there was any doubt she'd written **Golden Cobra** next to the arrow. I sometimes wonder what she thinks of us.

"An arrow pointing to a golden cobra," Madillo said, trying to keep her laughter in.

"Never mind about arrows. Yes, the golden cobra, who was warning the archaeologists not to enter the tomb. But did they listen? No. Do they ever listen? No. All for the sake of digging up a few jewels and messing around with the bones of dead people."

"But, Sister—" I began.

"Ah! When will I get through one day in peace without hearing from the Twin Who Likes to Say But?" she said, raising her eyes to the ceiling as if she was in agony.

I wasn't about to be put off.

"My mum says that Mr Carter died when he was an old man."

"So now your mother knows everything about medicine and archaeologists?" she asked. "I suppose she knows everything about nuns as well, does she, Bul-Boo? I think if you ask her you'll find she has an archaeologist in the family so she's biased."

In fact, my uncle, Mum's brother, is an archaeologist, but I didn't feel like admitting that to Sister.

"She might have one," I said. "Or she might not. Anyway, did Mr Carter die when he came out of the tomb? Straight away?"

"I wasn't there, thank God in the wild heavens above," Sister Leonisa replied. (I'll have to remember that she mentioned God today and write it down. It's very rare.) "But one of the archaeologists died, and at the exact moment that he collapsed in writhing agony, his dog howled to the heavens and it died too. They tried to say that this man died from a mosquito bite. Can you believe that, girls and boys, a silly little mosquito bite?"

"He probably got malaria," I couldn't resist saying. I don't know why but sometimes I seem unable to stop an argument with Sister even though I know it's pointless. Sister will never, ever admit that the other person is right. Mum said the other day that Sister is so disagreeable she wonders if she ever even manages to agree with herself.

Sister's face took on a smug look – the one I dread, that tells me she actually knows something I don't.

"You see, too-clever-for-anything Bul-Boo, this was an *Egyptian* mosquito, not a Zambian one. And the Egyptian mosquitoes don't give you malaria. Go and ask Doctor Lula about that. I know all about this, because I come from Caernarfon in Wales and it so

happens that this man, cursed to his death, was called Lord Carnarvon."

That was the first time any of us had heard she was from Wales. I'd always thought she was from Zambia, and Madillo and Fred say she's not from anywhere real. Madillo says she was made in a nun factory but that something went just a little bit wrong with the batch, which would explain why she is like she is. And then the school got her for a special discount. Fred says he's pleased it wasn't a Buy One, Get One Free offer, otherwise there'd be two of them and he'd be the favourite of both.

"Anyway," Sister continued, "these same archaeologists, the ones that didn't die, came to Zambia. Not satisfied with digging up Egypt, they came to make a mess of this country. The first place they headed for was Ng'ombe Ilede. The home of poor little Bukoko the Tick. And there they found two graveyards – one for all the rich people and one for all the poor people. It was easy to see why all the rich people had died. They were so weighed down by all their jewellery that they couldn't stand up any longer. So they fell to the ground in a heap of jewels and died. Which they deserved because they were so greedy. Death by jewellery – be careful of that, boys and girls, it's a nasty one.

"Then there was the other graveyard, for poor people. They had no jewellery at all. They died because

they were so exhausted from having to bury all the heavy rich people. Those people I feel sorry for. They didn't deserve it."

She looked around the classroom. "So, what have you learnt today? Fred?"

He stood up to answer, and counted on his fingers. "Don't become an archaeologist, don't wear jewellery, and if rich people die, don't dig deep graves for them otherwise you'll get exhausted and die yourself."

Sister clapped her hands. "Very good, Fred. You'll go a long way. One day your daddy is going to come to me and say, 'Thank you, Sister, you saved my boy's life.'"

Fred looked at her blankly. Rightly so, as he hadn't known his life had ever been in danger.

"Now," she said, "will the rest of you stand up to say goodbye."

We chanted, "Goodbye, Sister Leonisa, we wish you the best things in life and in death."

"And goodbye to you too, each and every one of you. I wish you all the best in life and in death."

Sister says we have to say this just in case she dies before she sees us again. She doesn't normally reply. I wish she hadn't today.

Perhaps Mum and Dad are right about her being morbid.

FRED

Talking to Girls

I seem to make a habit of being the favourite of grumpy old people. Like Sister Leonisa and Nokokulu. All it means is that they notice you more, and that's never a good thing. Nokokulu never notices Joseph and he's quite happy about that. He says it's because he has the power to make himself entirely invisible to her. I don't believe him.

I've never really been properly scared of Nokokulu, not in the way Madillo is, even though I think she's a witch. Witches don't have to be scary. Bul-Boo says there's no scientific proof that Nokokulu's a witch, but she's not always right. And scientific proof wouldn't do you much good if you were in the middle of being turned into a chameleon.

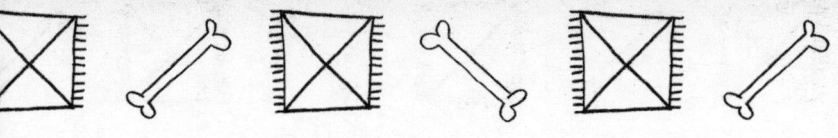

But — and it's a big but - one thing you do need around Nokokulu is caution. You learn caution every day with her. You have to, because you never know what she's going to do. I think it must be nice to be her, as she doesn't really care about anything much — not what she looks like, what she does, what she says or who she says it to.

For example, the way she dresses. She just wraps herself up in layers and layers of cloths. We call them *chitenge* and most normal people just wear one, as a skirt or a dress. Not Nokokulu. She wears as many as she feels like, wrapped around her in all sorts of different ways. As if we lived at the North Pole, not Zambia, where it's never cold. When she gets bored of one of her *chitenge* she unwraps it and rolls it into a tight little ball and leaves it wherever she happens to be when she takes it off. Perhaps near a stone. Or in a tree. Or on the birdbath. And she always mutters under her breath when she does it, as if she's saying, "Just stay here for a bit. I'll be back for you."

The problem is, she never does go back, and Mum then finds them all over the garden. The first time she found one she took it from its place in the tree and handed it to Nokokulu, saying, "I think you left this in the tree, Mama."

"Yes," Nokokulu said. "I did."

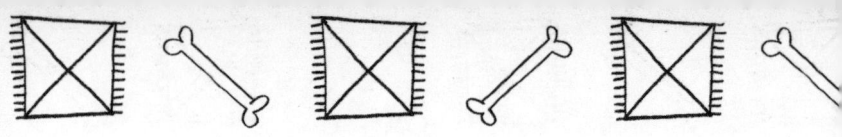

You can see the full stops when Nokokulu speaks, as if they're in the air. It means there's nothing more for anyone to say. But Mum doesn't always understand that.

"So, here it is," Mum said, as if Nokokulu was blind.

"I can see it."

A small frown appeared on Mum's face. "Well," she said, "would you like it back?"

"If I wanted it back I would not have left it in the tree. Did I ask you to bring it to me?"

"No, Mama, but…"

Before Mum could finish her sentence Nokokulu had turned her back to her and started whistling. If I was Mum I might have imagined she was whistling, "Oh, why did my darling grandson marry this silly woman from England who pesters me so." I don't know if that's what Mum heard, but she went and put the bundle back in the tree pretty quickly and since then has never moved another one. Last time I counted there were seventeen bundles scattered around the garden rotting away.

I am also careful to avoid trips in Nokokulu's yellow car. I'm not doing very well with that at the moment. I suppose I ought to be relieved that at least she can see over the steering wheel now because she has five cushions stacked up on her seat.

The first time we went driving with her was on her birthday when Dad gave her the car, and he suggested

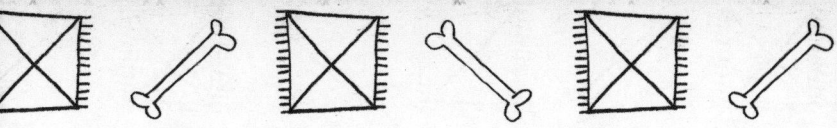

she took her great-grandsons out for a test drive.

"But Dad," Joseph said, "you're her grandson. We're only her great-grandsons. You have a turn first."

It was a good try, but it failed.

I waited for Mum to protest, but no. She just said, "Go on, boys, you enjoy yourselves. Look after Nokokulu. You're a big boy now, Freddy – I'm depending on you."

I was convinced on that day that in her previous life Mum had been a member of an English tribe who regarded it as their duty to kill their firstborn sons once they reached the age of ten. She just stood there waving to us and smiling.

Joseph, of course, jumped into the back, so the passenger seat next to Nokokulu was gapingly empty. She patted it and did that animal thing of baring her teeth at me while pretending to smile. I had no choice – my parents had abandoned me in my hour of need. I climbed in.

As we drove slowly out of the gate I looked back at them waving in unison as the car disappeared from their view. I could not be absolutely sure but I thought I detected an air of relief shimmering around their heads.

We survived that trip but it took a *very* long time. Dad told me afterwards that he had unwittingly bought the car from a known criminal so people knew the car. Unwittingly? I don't think so, but it certainly explains

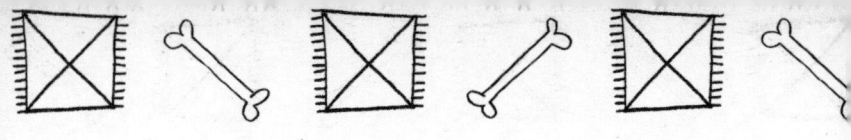

why no one hooted as Nokokulu drove at about twenty miles an hour.

She took us out towards Leopard's Hill and past the old cemetery.

"You know, boys," she said, "this cemetery has run out of empty ground. Run out completely. So by the time you're buried, they'll have to dig up a grave of some old person and squash you in beside them. You'll be buried for eternity with someone you don't know."

"What about when *you* die?" I asked.

"Me, Chiti? What did I tell you?"

"That dying is a waste of time."

"Yes."

"But if it's a waste of time for you, why not for us?"

"Because you, silly little boys, always waste time."

With that she went back to humming away to herself as if we weren't there and turned around to drive back home.

Hopefully for this trip to Ng'ombe Ilede she'll be mainly in a good mood. If she's in a good mood she ignores you. And if she's not at least I'll know that Bul-Boo and Madillo are there in the boot. Nothing too bad can happen if they're around, although I can't stop thinking about the Man-Beast. Nokokulu could be talking about the kryptops, I suppose, but that's been extinct for millions of years. It's Number Three on

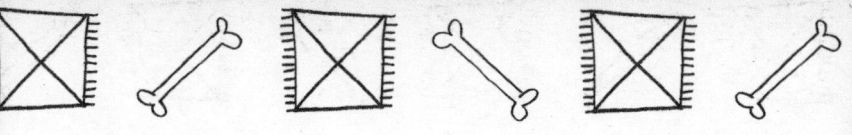

Sister Leonisa's list of Top Ten Monsters, because, as she says, "Just imagine how great it would be to meet a two-legged hyena," which is what the kryptops looks like. She has a funny idea of great.

If the twins do manage to come on this trip and *if* I manage to spend time with Bul-Boo on my own, I am not going to do what I did last time.

That time I proceeded to tell her, in great detail, about the time the whole Zambian soccer team was killed in a plane crash. She knew about it anyway – there isn't one person in Zambia who doesn't – but no one knows about it as well as I do. I thought (wrongly) that Bul-Boo might be impressed by my extensive knowledge. It was when I started listing off all the names that she started to look bored.

If Bul-Boo and I do happen to get onto the subject of soccer, at least this time I'll have good news for her, as our team, Chipolopolo, are now the champions of the Africa Cup of Nations. In fact we won the championship in the exact same place where the plane crashed all those years ago. Well, not the exact same place, because that would be in the sea, but in the city where the plane took off from. That's something.

Sometimes though it's hard to know what another person will find interesting. Especially if that person's a girl.

BUL-BOO

Goldfish Training

Mum was not very talkative when she came in today, but she cheered up a bit when we told her Sister's archaeologist story. I still tell her those kinds of stories, although some of the others I edit. Maybe she cheered up because she was looking for little things to help her not think about the big thing that was worrying her, i.e. the missing patients. And I learnt that one part of the story was true – mosquitoes in Egypt aren't malaria mosquitoes. Sister sometimes, I suppose, gets something right.

After supper we went up to our room to pack for our sleepover. I felt terrible about lying, but it was too late to change our minds now. We had to go so that Fred wasn't on his own.

Madillo didn't seem too worried.

"Fred says that there may not be a Man-Beast in Ng'ombe Ilede, that maybe he didn't hear properly. He thinks Nokokulu might have said 'manatee', not 'Man-Beast'," she said. "And of course it would be impossible for a manatee to turn up in Zambia every forty years to eat people."

"Unlike a Man-Beast?" I said. "There are loads of those wandering around."

Madillo ignored my eminently sensible intervention.

"When he first told us I thought he was making it all up, but he did look scared, didn't he?"

I had to agree. "He did actually. But he could have been pretending to look scared. He's quite a good actor."

Which is true.

"He once told me that his grandmother – you know, the one that never was his grandmother, because she died before he was born – was in fact eaten by a hyena," Madillo said.

"Who told him that?"

"Well, no one told him, but he heard his dad one day talking about a man-eating hyena and he heard the word 'mum' in the conversation, so he worked it out."

"If Fred overheard the words 'frog' and 'brother' in the same conversation he'd turn the frog into a poisonous spitting toad and have his brother blinded before

you know it," I said. "He's the master of worst possible scenarios."

"Well, it is strange that he's never been told what really happened to his granny. You have to admit that," Madillo pointed out. "Mum and Dad never keep things like that from us."

That is also true and sometimes I wish they would.

"I think," Madillo said, "that they wanted to protect him from developing a phobia about hyenas."

"Surely that would be a good phobia, as it might prevent you from being killed by one? I think they just didn't want him having bad dreams about it, if that was what happened at all."

"Maybe. I wish he hadn't told me though, because you know how hyenas' jaws are stronger than any other creature's, even a lion's? Can you imagine a young version of Nokokulu being crunched by this huge hyena, like a dog with a bone? Her legs sticking out one side and her head the other? Horrible."

"I hope you didn't say that to Fred!" I said, knowing that the answer was probably going to be yes. Or silence, which is as good as a yes.

I had my answer. Madillo just looked at the ground.

When we said goodbye to Mum and Dad I gave them really, really big hugs. If I were them I might have been a little suspicious. But they're not easily suspicious,

because we don't normally give them reason to be. Today they should have been.

Fred was sitting outside his house holding a round goldfish bowl scattered about with frangipani flowers. In between the flowers I could see two very dead goldfish. He had only had them for a little while – since his parents had decided that the only pets he couldn't kill were ones that could swim.

"What happened?" I asked.

"She cursed them, just like all the rest."

"You weren't trying to teach them to do tricks or anything?" I said suspiciously.

"Well, just small things. You know, like you see on TV where they get dolphins to throw balls to each other. Only these two weren't very good at it. Then when I got home from school they were dead. I am never having another pet in my whole life, at least not as long as Nokokulu is alive."

"Why the flowers?" Madillo asked, trying hard not to laugh.

Fred looked at her, debating whether or not she deserved a reply. "Funeral. Flowers. You know?"

"Sorry, Fred," she said. "I'm not laughing at the goldfish dying, that's sad, it just looks weird you sitting here with a bowl full of flowers. Sort of like a meditating guru."

Although Fred doesn't really know how to handle pets he does love them, so we both helped him bury the goldfish in his ever-expanding pet cemetery. He has created it as far away as possible from Nokokulu's small house at the back of their garden. It's under the lemon tree that his mother planted, in the corner of the garden near the front gate. Fred says that it's a nice-smelling part of the garden, so he knows they will all be happy there. It didn't seem right to point out that they were all dead and had lost their sense of smell.

We went to bed early as we had set our alarm for seven o'clock to make sure we'd be in the car before Nokokulu was up.

"We've already packed the tent and things like that," Fred said after he'd laid down.

"The tent?" Madillo and I repeated at exactly the same time.

"It's just in case of emergencies. You know, if there is a flood or something and we can't get back," he said.

"It's only just the start of the rainy season. We're not going to have floods now."

"Well, Nokokulu just said we should pack it. For if we break down or something like that. And some food…"

"Fred, is there something you've forgotten to tell us?" I asked. I was starting to get a really bad feeling

about this. "Are you sure we're only going for one day?"

"No – I mean, no, I haven't forgotten to tell you anything. It's just that you never know with Nokokulu. You have to be prepared for anything."

That didn't make me feel any better.

"But I think it'll be OK. She'll want to be back for church on Sunday, so she won't stay longer."

"We only told Mum and Dad we were coming for one sleepover. We definitely can't stay longer!" I exclaimed. "What if they come over here looking for us?"

Fred and Madillo stared at me. "Stop panicking, Bul-Boo," Madillo said. "Fred's just imagining the worst, aren't you, Fred."

He nodded.

He was right to be imagining the worst with Nokokulu in charge.

"I'm not panicking," I said calmly. "I just want to be sure. I don't want Mum and Dad to be worried, because they've enough to be thinking about, that's all. And we have too. We need to be back here to carry on with the investigation."

"We will be," Fred said, ignoring my reference to the disappearing patients. "Forget what I said about the tent."

As if.

I waited until they were both asleep then wrote an entry in my notebook:

APPROACHES TO SOLVING A PROBLEM:

FRED
Just forget the problem ever existed

MADILLO
Pretend the problem is not as big as it seems

ME
Accept the inevitable and go to sleep

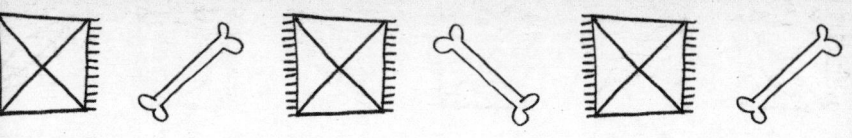

FRED

Nokokulu Versus the World

It was quiet in the house when we got up, as Mum and Dad sleep in on Saturdays. We were able to sneak out to the car without anyone seeing us. Luckily it was parked in the driveway, so our house was between the car and Nokokulu's house. There was no way she could see us.

I felt sorry for the twins having to get into the boot. It didn't look particularly comfortable. They had to climb in behind the tent as well as a huge suitcase Nokokulu had put in. When I lifted it out of the way it felt empty. I don't know what she was thinking bringing an empty suitcase.

The good thing about it was that it would hide them from view if anyone opened the boot. They are

quite small, the twins, and the back part of the yellow car is very large, so they fitted in OK. Bul-Boo says they're only small because they had to share the space in their mum's womb, which I suppose makes sense. Although I did tell them about a pair of really tall twins in *Guinness World Records* who grew to seven and a half feet tall. Bul-Boo just said, "I pity their mother," and Madillo shrugged and added, "Well, they're American." As if that somehow explained everything.

After I shut the boot I crept back into the house and back to bed so that Nokokulu wouldn't get suspicious.

At exactly eight o'clock she came and banged on my door. "We're late, Chiti. Get out of bed now, you lazy boy, and we'll go." She must have woken everyone up with her shouting but none of them came to see us off.

When I got downstairs Nokokulu handed me a sandwich. "We'll eat in the car, otherwise the darkness will come and we won't be able to find our way."

If the darkness had come then, it would have been the shortest day in the recorded history of Zambia: the sun had only been up for a couple of hours. But I didn't tell her that. She already knew it, she was just looking for something impatient to say to me.

As we walked towards the car my heart started thumping really loudly. If she found the twins now we'd

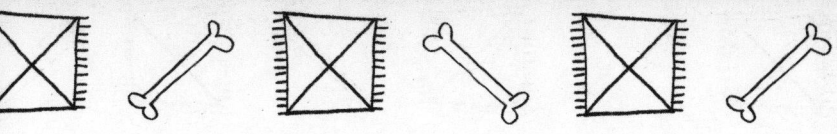

all be dead meat. She turned round and looked at me, as if she could hear my terror. But she said nothing.

We both got in, and once the doors were shut I gave a big sigh of relief.

Too big as it turned out.

"You have something you want to say, Chiti? Where's your map?" Nokokulu said.

The map. That I had carefully packed in the bag that was now in the boot. I had to think quickly.

"Sorry, Nokokulu, I'll jump out and get it. You relax," I said, opening my door.

"Me, relax? You think I'm an old woman who needs to relax?" she said, opening her door too.

I jumped out of the car and ran round to the boot. As I opened it a hand reached out and gave me the map. Along with it I heard a Madillo giggle, which was not very helpful. I slammed the boot shut and ran back to my seat before Nokokulu had got properly out of the car. Luckily she *is* actually an old woman and a little bit stiff.

"You can read this map?" Nokokulu said as we headed out of the driveway.

"Yes. Sister taught us in school," I said.

Sister was supposed to teach us about maps when she taught us Geography. But she said that road maps were stupid and how were you supposed to know where you

were going if there were no obvious things like trees or gates or buildings on them – things that would help you to know you were heading in the right direction. Bul-Boo told her there was north, south, west and east to do that, but Sister ignored her.

"You think that makes me feel better," Nokokulu said, "hearing that that mad nun taught you about maps?"

I think Nokokulu and Sister would get on really well, because they're both a little bit mad, but I decided not to say that.

"I know how to get to Kariba, anyway, and it's near there," I told her.

"The sun is near the moon but that doesn't help much, does it, boy? I know where we're going but I want you to direct me. It's part of your training."

Training for what?

The first part of the journey was torture. Nokokulu drove so slowly. She said that the car took time to warm up its engine and if we rushed it might give up on us. Imagine if all cars needed that long to warm up!

It took us almost an hour just to get to Chilanga. That means we were driving at twenty kilometres an hour along the Great North Road, and behind us was a long line of truck drivers hooting and flashing. If I'd been driving I would have felt pretty embarrassed, but Nokokulu didn't.

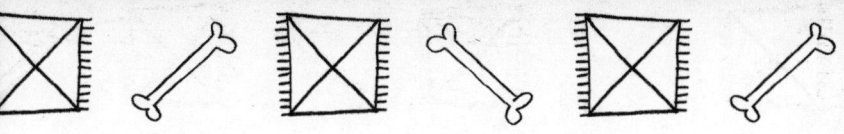

"Ha! They can hoot and flash their silly lights, I don't care. What's the big hurry? It's Saturday morning – they should all still be in bed. What'd you say, boy?" she asked, turning to look at me.

If I hadn't answered she might have carried on asking and looking at me and forgetting to watch the road, so I said, "You're right, Nokokulu, they should all have stayed in bed."

Nokokulu just ignored my answer and stuck her arm out of the car window to shake her fist at a truck driver who had dared to pass her. I sometimes think she sees her life as a replay of David and Goliath – Nokokulu versus the world.

Anyway, once we got to Chilanga and were passing Munda Wanga gardens she decided that right then would be a good time to go in, despite the fact that the gates were not only closed but padlocked. Even if she does have bad eyesight she must have seen that. The gates are not invisible – they are painted red and yellow.

Before I could shout out, we hit the gates. The sound was very loud. At the same moment I heard a squeal from the back. It must have been Madillo because I've never heard Bul-Boo make a noise like that.

"Stupid, stupid Munda Wanga!" Nokokulu shouted. "Why do you have a sign that says 'Visitors Welcome', then chase the visitors away? What's the point of closed

gates? And what was that funny noise? Like a small pig? Did we hit an animal?"

"I didn't see anything," I said quickly.

"Neither did I, silly boy. I said I *heard* something. Listen," she said, tilting her head to one side and totally ignoring the fact that we had just crashed into the park gates.

I just shook my head. "I can't hear anything."

"Deaf like your father, that's all."

With that she reversed and drove back out onto the road leaving behind us a pair of badly dented gates. I was worried about Bul-Boo and Madillo – what if something had happened to them? Maybe they'd been impaled on a tent peg and were lying there slowly bleeding to death.

I had to do something.

"Nokokulu, I need to pee. Now," I said, trying to sound desperate. Which wasn't hard, as I already had visions of them lying in a pool of blood, my premonition of doom finally come true.

"Use a bottle. There are empty ones behind the seat."

She's not only wicked; she's gross.

"I can't. I have to stop," I said. "Pull over. Please."

She turned to look at me.

"I'll stop, but only because I want to stretch my legs. And only for three minutes," she added.

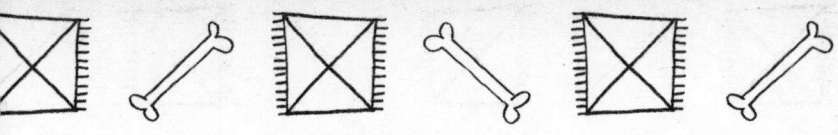

With that she pulled over into the dirt at the side of the road and skidded to a halt.

We both got out at the same time and she walked off into the bush before I could say anything. I ran round to the boot and opened it. "You all right?" I whispered.

"Yes, we're fine. Shut the door," Bul-Boo whispered back.

I slammed it shut as Nokokulu reappeared.

"What are you doing, Chiti?" she said. "Peeing in the boot?"

I was sure that I heard giggles coming from the back.

"Just checking it was closed properly," I said.

"Now," she said as she climbed back in, "where are we going? I want instructions from my map reader for our next crash." Then she started laughing and banging the steering wheel as if she'd just won the prize for Best Joke in the World. On top of everything else she finds herself really funny. "You want to make me drive into the Kafue River, perhaps, Chiti? Then we can both be eaten by crocodiles. Or we could drive into an acacia tree and forget that behind it we might find an elephant trying to reach the pods for a feast? Ha!"

"Chirundu," I said, trying hard to ignore how irritated I was feeling. "We need to go to Chirundu."

"Ha! Chirundu. Stone trees," she said. "Stone people."

I knew there was a petrified forest near Chirundu,

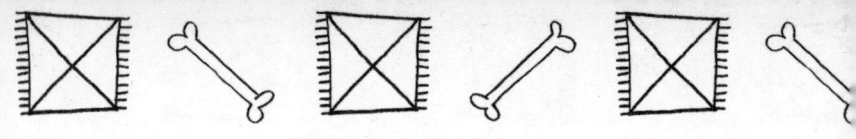

but I have never heard of petrified people. And I didn't really care. All I could think about was what had happened at Munda Wanga. What if there were cameras there and they had photographed our number plate? Perhaps the crocodiles would escape through the gap in the dented gates and make their way to town looking for human prey. If they attacked and killed anyone that would make us Accessories to Murder and the rest of our days would be spent in prison.

Nokokulu, probably the only *real* murderer among us, wouldn't get sent there because they'd take one look at her and think she was on her last legs (little do they know). Then the twins would get off because they're female and Dad says females never go to prison. So it'd be me. By myself. Rotting away in a cell, chained to the wall, marking off the days one by one. By the time they released me Bul-Boo would probably be married to someone else and she wouldn't even look at me.

Mind you, once Nokokulu discovers the twins in the back of the car, prison might seem like quite a nice place.

BUL-BOO

The Journey
of a Stubborn Old Woman

That was the longest journey of my whole life. Normally a trip to Kariba with Mum and Dad takes about two hours. We were squashed into the boot for more than *five*. The crash didn't help either, although at least it wasn't something crashing into the back of us.

From what I could hear, Nokokulu ignored any instructions Fred gave her, despite the fact that he was the Official Map Reader. It would almost have been better if he'd said nothing, or if he'd said the opposite of the direction she needed to take. Each time he said "Turn right here" she would turn left. If he said "Just carry straight on" she would make a turn, left or right, depending on what she felt like.

I don't know how many times I heard him say, "We

have only one turn to take, Nokokulu — only one, to Siavonga." But she didn't listen, and told him he must learn to read maps properly.

I drew this map in my black notebook while we were driving. It kept me busy at least.

NOKOKULU'S ROUTE
FRED'S MAP ROUTE

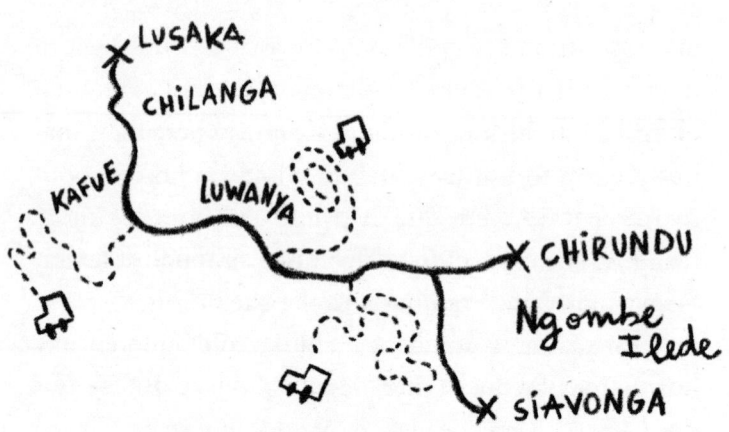

That's why it took five hours. I called it: The Journey of a Stubborn Old Woman.

The journey also took a long time because Nokokulu stops for food so often. Fred had put the food bag inside the car, not in the boot, so as well as

stopping to eat they snacked along the way. It wasn't very nice hearing eating noises when we couldn't have anything. Especially as we knew there'd be chocolate involved. Nokokulu says chocolate is good for your brain, so they always have loads of it at their house. I wish she'd tell Mum that.

When they made their first food stop it was only about ten o'clock and the car was already *boiling* hot. Madillo hates it when I say it's boiling hot, because she always imagines us in a giant *puga-puga* filled with boiling water, trying to climb out of the sides. I don't mean it literally, but Madillo has difficulty understanding the difference between meaning something literally and just using words to describe something.

It's Sister's fault really.

One day in class, when Sister was pretending to be a Science teacher, she said, "If you woke up one day and decided that it would be a good day for boiling frogs, how would you make sure they didn't jump out of your pot?"

We all sat and stared at her. I was about to say that I wouldn't want to boil frogs but that if I did I would put a lid on the pot. However, I didn't get the chance, because as usual she didn't actually want an answer from us.

"I'll tell you," she said. "You put the frog in cold

water and then you slowly heat it. The frog starts to enjoy it and doesn't realize that it's getting hotter and hotter, so he doesn't jump out. And, lo and behold, one boiled frog."

When I looked this up later to check if Sister was right (she wasn't), I also came across the fact that people have done experiments on frogs to prove the existence of a soul. As if a soul can be found. Even Sister Leonisa says the soul is an idea not a thing, and she's a nun. I don't mind if people believe in it, that's their business, but don't go boiling frogs and experimenting on them to find it. That's just cruel.

Madillo spent all of the journey drawing little Manga characters. She's very good at it, but they didn't look as good as they usually do because she was drawing in the dark and it wasn't a smooth ride. Some sections of the road are full of potholes and that didn't help.

Another downside to the journey taking so long was that I had time to think. That's not always a good thing. Even though I had been trying hard not to think about Mum's patients who had died, I couldn't help myself. Their names were stuck in my head. Especially Sonkwe's, as we had seen that photograph of him. My so-called investigation seemed to have come to a stand-still. I couldn't even call it an investigation as I was spending all my time trying not to think about it and

putting pretend suspects on a list, which meant that the other eight people were still in danger while I was stuck in the back of an old yellow car. And I couldn't really call my one and only suspect a real suspect as that would mean I thought Nokokulu was a serial killer, which I definitely didn't.

Luckily I had my *Book of Rocks* with me and a small clip-on light. That helped me pass some of the time and stop thinking. Fred and Madillo have never been especially interested in rocks – apart from batholiths, and that's only because Madillo says they sound like someone with a lisp trying to say "basilisks". She loves the idea that a basilisk can kill someone just by glancing in their general direction. She finds that more impressive than the fact that some of the granite rocks around Kafue are 3,000 million years old – in other words, three billion years old. How cool is that? Much cooler than a basilisk because it's actually true, not just made up.

After many more detours and arguments between Fred and Nokokulu we stopped again. Apparently the signpost for Ng'ombe Ilede was finally in view.

As she turned off the engine I heard Nokokulu announce, "We still have time before the sun sets. It is only when the sun sets that *he* comes out of hiding. We can rest now."

"What do you mean, Nokokulu?" asked Fred, a

mixture of terror and helplessness in his voice. "We all have to be back by evening. That's why we left early – you said that. And who's 'he'?"

"Never mind who 'he' is. Who is 'we all'?" said Nokokulu.

"I mean *me*. I have to be back – I've got soccer practice."

"You don't play soccer any more," she said.

That is true; I really, really don't know how Fred got to be such a poor liar.

"And we left early because that is when I decided to leave. Anything could have happened on the road. We could have sunk into one of the potholes and never come out again. One of the tyres could have exploded, and then you'd have had to walk many miles to a garage to get a new one. No more questions. We're here. We'll rest.

"If I start searching after the sun sleeps," she continued, almost talking to herself, "I will be done by the time he walks again. I can feel he is out there, the Man-Beast. But we are here now. His end is coming."

Fred was silent. Madillo gave a little squeak. For once in my life I felt like giving a very big squeak. None of this tied in with what I was investigating. At least I didn't think so. But something was definitely going to happen. She had a plan and it involved some kind of

beast that sounded completely terrifying.

Madillo grabbed my leg. I decided I would try Dad's trick of pretending everything was all right.

"The poor old lady," I whispered to her. "I think she has finally lost her marbles. Let's just play along and try to get home as soon as possible."

Madillo didn't answer.

"All right," Nokokulu said, "I'm going to sleep now. Chiti, you be quiet."

With that there was a clatter as she let her seat go back.

I held my breath and waited. Sure enough, within about three minutes the rumbling started. The loudest snores I had ever heard, so loud they shook the car.

Then I heard Fred carefully opening his door and coming round to the back of the car. He clicked open the boot and peered in at us mournfully, almost as if he expected us to be dead.

He pulled the large suitcase away, trying hard to be quiet, and we rolled forward, unwrapping our legs as best we could. We crouched down behind the car and I pulled him down next to us.

"How are we going to do this?" I whispered.

He shrugged his shoulders. We hadn't thought this far.

Madillo looked at me. "Come on, Bul-Boo," she said. "Think of something."

I sighed. Neither of them were going to be any use.

"Well…" I said, trying to think clearly.

"*Well* what?" Nokokulu's voice shouted, right next to my ear.

I jumped up.

There she was, on her hands and knees, like a ninja. She had somehow crept from her seat, round the car and sneaked up on us.

Madillo burst into loud noisy tears and stayed crouched down behind me. Fred looked stricken.

There was nothing we could say that would make this any better at all.

Nokokulu stood up.

"Where do these useless, useless, bad, wicked, stupid, smelly little children come from to torment me?" she shouted to the sky. "And YOU," she said as she turned to Fred and grabbed his ear. "Bad, bad boy. Very bad. As bad as a rotten pumpkin. As bad as a snake with no brain. Why?" she wailed, letting his ear go and falling to the ground in a little angry heap of *chitenges*, "why am I cursed in this way?"

Not one of us said a word.

She sat up and dusted herself off.

"And the doctors?" she said very quietly to me and Madillo. "The doctors know you are here?"

I shook my head.

A small grin appeared on her face. A small evil grin.

"Oh. Not good. Not good at all. Big, big trouble coming your way, *mpundu*. Big, big trouble."

As if we didn't know that already.

Madillo's sobs were subsiding but she remained hidden behind me

Fred was just looking at the ground muttering to himself under his breath.

Nokokulu heard him too.

"And now I have a great-grandson who talks to himself. No good will come of this I tell you. No good at all. There was a man in my village who always talked to himself and he quickly forgot how to talk to other people. No woman would marry him. Who wants a man who says nothing to anybody? Nobody, I tell you. So what did he do? He ran away from the village and they say he is living among the animals, because he has learnt how to talk to them. You want to become like that man, Chiti? You think one of these twins will marry a man who talks to himself?"

I felt so sorry for Fred. He looked like he'd rather be anywhere than here. I am very pleased that my relatives don't get cross with us in front of our friends. It's a horrible embarrassing thing.

Nokokulu stood up.

"Well, now you're here you'll just have to stay while I do my business. On my own," she added, looking at

Fred. "The Man-Beast would smell a lying boy from miles away. So. No silly singing or shouting. You do what I say, when I say it. No arguments. No laughing."

She didn't need to add that one in. I wasn't sure any of us would ever laugh again.

"I have work to do tonight. You three will stay in the tent while I do my work."

"Tonight?" I ventured. "We're staying here tonight?"

Her grin reappeared.

"*I'm* staying here tonight. You want to go home, you can go. I don't think it was me who invited you here!"

Maybe Fred hadn't been exaggerating after all. Everything he had ever said about her was probably true. Imagine her being quite happy to let us walk off on our own in the middle of the bush!

"Not going?" she asked, watching as neither me nor Madillo went anywhere. "Fine. We will all stay here tonight then. I have two tents – one for Chiti, one for me – and I have food. You can stay with Chiti in his tent and try and get some sleep in between all the talking he does to himself."

With that, she turned and got back into the driver's seat, shouting as she went, "Get in the car now. We have only one mile more then we will be at The Place of the Cow Who Lies Down." She started up the engine and all three of us ran and jumped into the car.

Everything had gone wrong. Absolutely everything. Now we were stuck here for the night, when Mum and Dad were expecting us back. When we didn't arrive they'd phone Fred's parents, who would tell them we had gone home early that morning. Then they'd contact the police and a huge search party would be sent out. They'd probably think we'd been abducted by the same person who had killed Sonkwe and Thandiwe.

That's the problem with making something up. It grows. One small lie leads to another and another till there's nothing left for you to do but lie full time. Imagine being condemned to a life like that? You'd wake up in the morning and have to try to remember all the lies you'd told the day before just to make sure you didn't make any mistakes.

Terrible.

Leabharlanna Poiblí Chathair Baile Átha Cliath
Dublin City Public Libraries

BUL-BOO

Storm Clouds Gathering

The car was completely silent as we travelled the last mile to the huge sideways baobab tree. Madillo sat and drew a tent with three miserable faces looking out of it and giant black clouds above it. Fred just stared straight ahead. I checked my phone and saw that I actually had three bars of signal on it. I considered phoning Dad or Mum. They'd be mad, there was no question about that, but it couldn't possibly be worse than the night we were facing, camping with an angry Nokokulu who was here to search for some unknown two-legged half man, half beast creature. She had gone back to the top of my list of suspects. I was now considering writing her full name in. In pen.

But if I phoned Dad and he came to fetch us it

would mean us leaving Fred here on his own with her. We couldn't do that. We couldn't let him down like that.

Nokokulu braked hard and the car skidded on the dirt road. "Wait here," she said to us. "I will be back. Don't talk."

We all just looked at one another. Right now there was no way we were going to disobey her.

I looked down at my phone again. Still a few bars. I decided to put off phoning and go online and resume my search instead.

"That's really strange," I whispered, forgetting the instruction.

"What?" asked Fred.

"Well, I've been searching for something here, in Zambia, and a US site keeps coming up."

"If there aren't many instances of the thing you're searching for in Zambia," said Fred, who liked an excuse to show how much he knew about the Web, "then sites located elsewhere will come up."

"But there are a *lot* of instances of this in Zambia."

"Then you can be sure that the US site makes some reference to Zambia," said Fred with authority. "It might not be on the front page, it could be a link or a meta tag, but most likely there's text on that site that says something about Zambia. You should look through every page."

My phone signal was failing as the Ratsberg and Wrath site started to show itself on my little screen. I couldn't see anything obviously linked to Zambia at first, then as I was about to exit I saw a funny link right at the bottom of the splash page: **HOPE IN AFRICA!** I clicked the link, but then the signal went altogether. I asked the others to check their phones. Madillo's of course was out of charge. Fred had no signal either.

Nokokulu arrived at my window and banged on it. "Open up, *mpundu!*" she shouted. "I don't know why you think these silly phone things will work in this place where powerful spirits rule the air and the earth? This tree," she said pointing to the baobab, "this tree doesn't want to hear any city noises here. You understand?"

She shook her head sorrowfully. "No sense, no sense in the brains of children in this century. Now, out, out all of you. You," she said, pointing at me, "take the tents out of the boot and put them up. The biggest one is mine and I want it near the tree. And you, Chiti, when the tents are fixed, you get my suitcase out of the car and put it into my tent."

I'm not sure why Madillo escaped any work, but she did. It was probably because she had still not uttered a single word so Nokokulu had forgotten she was even there.

I wasn't about to ask questions, anyway. I just got the

tents out of the boot and started to put them up. Fred looked like he wanted to help, but because he hadn't been instructed to he just stood to one side watching. He was right – we didn't need any more trouble from Nokokulu.

Madillo sat down near where I was working until Nokokulu shouted at her, "Hey, small twin, you know if you sit in the dirt too long you'll get worms in your bum? Mad Girl, if the worms find a way in, they'll crawl up to your brain and make you even madder."

I think Nokokulu is missing that switch in her head which stops parents, grandparents and especially great-grandparents from being rude to other people's children. She just doesn't have it.

Last time she called Madillo "Mad Girl", Fred asked her not to and she said that our mum and dad shouldn't have given her a name which starts with "mad". Sometimes she shortens my name to Boo and thinks it's really funny to shout it out as if she's giving me a fright.

Madillo just got up without saying anything and went and stood next to Fred. As they were standing there watching me a dark cloud appeared, as if from nowhere. The sky had been bright and sunny all morning, but now the cloud blocked all that out. It was definitely a thundercloud and I saw Fred looking at it and thinking the same thing. He's not fond of thunderstorms. He has a

theory that he is going to be killed by a bolt of lightning – and that's not so far-fetched because a lot of people do die each year in Zambia from being struck by lightning. One of the reasons Fred stopped playing soccer was because he read that story about a soccer team in Congo where all eleven players were killed by lightning. He said no one from the other team was killed. After reading that nothing would persuade him to go back to playing.

Fred's father decided it would be a good idea for Fred to conquer his fear of lightning by doing a project on it. This was probably the worst idea he'd ever had. Fred called his project "Lightning Can Strike Twice, In Fact it Can Strike Seven Times", and it was about a man in America called Roy Sullivan who was struck by lightning seven times and each time he survived. He then apparently got so tired of all this that he shot himself. The worst part of the story (apart from the fact that he shot himself) is that one of the times he was struck he was travelling in his car, which is supposed to be a really safe place to be during a thunderstorm. The results of Fred's project were: (a) he got more scared of lightning and (b) Sister Leonisa decided to tell us some lightning stories of her own.

One of these took place in a church in a small town in Italy where lightning struck the steeple of a church. The trouble was that in the basement of the church

there were a hundred barrels of gunpowder. These were ignited by the lightning strike and a huge explosion destroyed everyone in the town.

After telling us this Sister asked, "So, what's the moral of that story?"

Because there's always a moral with Sister Leonisa.

"Don't store gunpowder in the basement?" Madillo said, which seemed logical.

Sister shook her head sadly. "Anyone else?"

"Don't build steeples?" Fred tried.

"No, Fred, that's silly," Sister said. "Nowhere is safe. That's the moral, girls and boys. Nowhere, not even a church. Especially not a church."

We all went silent then, as that was just confusing. Firstly, it wasn't a moral. Secondly, why was she, a nun, warning us against going to church?

She suddenly looked a bit confused herself, as if she'd forgotten why she was telling us this.

Anyway.

I finished putting up the tents and Fred ran to the car to get Nokokulu's suitcase. He carried it easily because it was so light.

Madillo, who had now found her voice, whispered to me, "She probably brought it with her so she could put Fred's dead body in it to bring back. Now we've foiled her evil plan."

I didn't answer. Why did she keep putting words like "dead body" and "murder" in the same sentence as "Fred"?

"You go and have a rest in your tent now," Nokokulu told us. "I will call you when I need you. And remember, no noise. You must not wake up the ancestors."

She seemed to have forgotten that all the bodies that were buried here had been dug up many years ago. If we wanted to wake them we'd have to go and make a noise outside the Livingstone Museum. But none of us was going to point that out to her. We were all relieved, I think, to be able to escape into the tent, where we could talk without her listening in. We needed to decide what to do.

When we got into the tent, before either Madillo or I could say anything Fred blurted out, "She's evil. She planned all along that we'd stay here. My own great-grandmother, lying to me." He sat down on one of the rolled-up sleeping bags. "And those disappearances, Aunt Kiki and the others, I bet she's behind them. She's so ... mean sometimes. And rude."

"It's not her," I said.

The others looked at me. Neither of them were in the mood right then to hear someone defending Nokokulu.

"I'm not saying she's not evil or anything,"

I explained, "just that she's no longer the prime suspect in the abductions."

There I was, talking about the disappearances as abductions, like Madillo.

"So who is, if it's not her?" asked Fred, looking a little relieved. I think in a funny way he does love Nokokulu. It's just that sometimes she makes herself unlovable. Like today.

"The primary suspects have just been reinstated," I said, getting a little carried away with myself. "I just know."

"You just know?" Madillo said. "What's that supposed to mean?"

"I'm not going to go into the details now," I said. "But trust me. We will have a peaceful day and night here. Knowing Nokokulu, she's probably brought really good food with her. If her temper improves, she might even share it with us. And when we get home tomorrow I will prove to you that somebody else is to blame for the disappearances, which means we'll be able to find Aunt Kiki and the others."

I was quite wrong about the peaceful night part.

BUL-BOO

Life's Sorrows

Madillo and Fred both looked at me as if I'd lost my mind, which was understandable really as I wasn't exactly giving them much to go on. Just that I had a strong hunch that was growing by the minute. The hunch was based on evidence; I just didn't want to talk to them about it till I really knew.

"Your phone had a bar of signal over by the car," said Madillo. "Maybe we ought to phone home and tell them the truth, then they'll come and fetch us."

This wasn't like Madillo. She likes adventure better than anyone I know. Certainly more than I do. Nowhere spooks her. But something here was spooking her badly.

Before I could respond we suddenly heard a strange sound from the other tent. Fred looked at me and

Madillo, who shrugged. I crept out of our tent towards the noise. The others followed. First we heard the snores. Then they stopped abruptly and Nokokulu started talking. Very fast.

"She's in a trance," whispered Madillo. "She's casting a spell."

"Or maybe she's just talking in her sleep," I said.

Nokokulu's voice grew softer. She was speaking in Bemba.

"When you took my flower away from me I should have come after you. Now you are taking the next one. This time I am here. If it's me you want, I am here. If you will spare my Kiki, you can have me without a fight. My powers are passing to my boy. You will not be able to touch him. He is beyond your reach. He is here to witness. He has come to take Kiki home."

We were all quiet. Fred had tears in his eyes. I looked down at my shoes. Suddenly Nokokulu had gone back to being a very sad old lady. Who knew how many sorrows a person could pick up in a hundred years. My mum was much younger than Nokokulu and she already had sorrows. Why had I never thought of it like that before? The reason Fred's great-granny was bent down and crotchety was because of the load of life's sorrows she was carrying.

Of course that still didn't make her a very nice old

lady. All of us knew enough about Nokokulu not to expect her to come out of the tent transformed into someone gentle and kind. But she was definitely not our serial killer.

"We must stay the night now," said Fred quietly. "I don't want our parents coming here to take us all back before Nokokulu has had a chance to do whatever it is she thinks she must do. I owe her that much after betraying her in my head, thinking the worst of her."

This was a longer, more serious speech than I'd ever heard from Fred. It made me feel sort of proud of him.

"I agree with Fred," I said, dismissing the pleading look from Madillo. "But we still have the problem that Mum and Dad are expecting us home tonight. We'll have to tell them we're staying over at Fred's again."

"What about us?" Madillo asked. "We're not beyond the reach of the Man-Beast. Chiti may be protected but we're not. That's why she didn't want us to come."

It was strange to hear her call Fred "Chiti". Neither Fred nor I commented. She had a strange look about her.

"Don't think like that," I said firmly. "She's just confused by her regrets. By tomorrow she will have met her dreaded Man-Beast in her sleep and sorted things out with him. Then we can all go home and sort out the real demons."

"But why does she think he's taken Aunt Kiki? She

was living in Lusaka. It doesn't make any sense."

"No, it doesn't," I agreed. "She's just upset and it's made her muddled."

"My phone battery is flat," interrupted Madillo, "and if I make the call I don't think I'll be able to stop myself from asking Mum to come and collect us straight away."

Which was her way of saying that I had to be the one who phoned. As usual.

Mum sounded tired when she picked up the phone. She had been called out to the clinic during the night and was still half asleep so she didn't ask any questions – which was lucky, because I'm sure if she'd been properly awake she would have known from the sound of my voice that something was not quite right.

I had gone to stand by the car to make the call and when I came back to the tents I saw that Fred and Madillo had wandered off to look at the strange lying down baobab tree.

"Hey!" I shouted, running over to them.

"How did it go?" Madillo asked.

"It's done, that's all. And you two were supposed to be waiting here in case Nokokulu woke up."

"She's still asleep. Can't you hear?" Madillo said.

She was right – the snores were rumbling again.

Not for long though.

"Ha!" came Nokokulu's voice from her tent. "Ha!

You talking about me, Chiti and your two twin friends?
What are you up to?"

It was as if, even though she had been fast asleep, she
had heard every word we'd said.

"We're going to climb the tree, Nokokulu," Fred
said quickly.

"And the lightning?" she said.

At that moment, the large black cloud moved across
the sun, blocking it out almost completely.

FRED

The Purple-striped Burrowing Praying Mantis

I had almost forgotten about the lightning. Almost. I know Bul-Boo doesn't believe that Nokokulu has magical powers but it was not a coincidence that just as she said the word, the cloud blocked out the sun. I sometimes think my great-granny likes scaring me. She said to Dad once that it's good for children to be scared now and again, otherwise they'll think there's nothing to be scared of.

There is no danger whatsoever of me growing up imagining that there is nothing in this world to be afraid of.

Last Sunday Nokokulu brought a wooden coffin-shaped box into the kitchen and put it on the table. She told me and Joseph that inside it was a very small

dead ancestor and that if we dared open it we would be cursed for infinity. I stared at the small coffin (it was only big enough to hold a cat) and knew that I wouldn't ever touch it. I didn't even want my breath to touch the outside of it in case it thought I was approaching with the thought of opening it.

Joseph is different from me. He doesn't talk much and he doesn't really believe in things he can't see.

Nokokulu looked at him. She knows what he's like. "And if you open it, Joseph Muŋwiŋwi Mwamba, it won't only be you who is cursed, it will be your older brother as well." She then left the room.

Dad once described her as "wily". She was being very wily then, because even if I had to knock Joseph to the ground and make him unconscious, I wouldn't let him near the box.

His middle name is not Muŋwiŋwi by the way. That means "mosquito". And the letter in it, ŋ, is a letter only found in Bemba. You pronounce it ng. I like it. And he is a bit like a mosquito when he decides to be annoying.

We never found out what was in the box, but Dad said it was most likely chocolates.

"Nokokulu," I said, "if a storm comes we all have to stay in the car away from the tree."

I tried hard to keep my voice deep. At the moment it is in the process of breaking, and breaking is the right

word for it. I never really know what it's going to do. I like the sound of my new voice. I just wish it would stop running away and leaving this awful noise in its place.

"Chiti, stop speaking in a girl's voice," she said. "You want me to make the storm go away? I can do it, just like that – *hocus pocus, psika psoka.*"

She made her hands into little claw-like shapes in front of her and started muttering magic words. Well, they sounded like magic words – they weren't in any of the languages I know. Some days I wish I had been born into a family that was witch- and ancestor-free. An instant family with parents who were never born but who just appeared one day, fully trained to be nice fair parents and that was it.

"Yes, yes, please, Nokokulu, make it go away!" a voice said behind me.

I didn't even need to turn around to see that it was Madillo speaking. Identical twins they may be but I know how different they are. Not in a million years would Bul-Boo ask Nokokulu to make a spell. If Nokokulu lived with them instead of with me I just know Madillo would make her do spells all day long.

I regret ever telling Madillo that Nokokulu is a powerful witch. I think what sealed it was when I told her about when she magicked a man into growing horns on his head that just grew and grew until he could no

longer stand up with the pure weight of them.

All the witch things I know about my great-granny are what she has told me. It's not that I don't believe she's a witch; it's just that sometimes I wonder. Maybe it's because of Bul-Boo. I think I'm going to ask Nokokulu to prove it to me one day.

Except not today.

Nokokulu looked at Madillo. "For you, Mad Girl, I will chase the storm away. But I want my boy to ask me as well."

I took a deep breath. "Please, Nokokulu, make the storm go away with one of your spells," I said very quietly, wishing that Bul-Boo wasn't there listening.

And just like that, away it went. I can't prove it was Nokokulu, but five minutes after she'd muttered something and done a funny little dance, the clouds cleared and the sun shone.

"Coincidence," Bul-Boo whispered to me. "Pure coincidence."

It might have been, but even Bul-Boo sounded like she was trying to persuade herself.

"Now can we go and climb the Sleeping Cow tree?" Madillo asked. "That was brilliant, Nokokulu, a perfect spell."

"I know it was brilliant. That's what I do, brilliant things."

Nokokulu always answers a compliment about herself with another one – about herself!

I wished I could tell her about my feeling of doom, perhaps then she'd make it go away like the clouds. But I didn't feel like hearing her laugh at me. I decided just to keep it to myself and hope that we would escape from there without anything bad happening.

If I was Hindu, according to what Sister Leonisa taught us I would believe that if I did good things in life then good things would happen to me, but if I did bad things then bad things would happen, and in my next life I might come back as a crab or a tick. Or something worse. I don't think I agree. I mean, bad things happen all the time to people who are good. Say if you look at the soccer team who crashed into the Atlantic. What had they done apart from being the best ever soccer players? Or Aunt Kiki? Most of all Aunt Kiki. She never did anything bad to anybody and then she got sick and disappeared. How could anyone say she deserved that?

I couldn't think of anything that I'd done in my life that would mean I deserved whatever disaster was about to befall us if my prediction of doom was correct. Mind you, Sister may have been wrong about what Hinduism teaches, as she's wrong about most things. Dad says that Hinduism is at least a peaceful religion, because

it doesn't spend its life telling everyone else that they should be Hindus.

"Run, run, then. Climb the tree. But I don't know what you think you're going to find. There's nothing to see, only a fallen-down tree and a silly monument," Nokokulu said.

We all looked at her. She can be very confusing.

"What about the dead ancestors?" I asked.

"What d'you think, boy, that they'll be walking around here?"

She laughed. Loudly. Which was not necessary – we were right next to her.

"No," I said. "I know where the things they dug up from here are, the bones and the jewels and everything. They're in Livingstone, in the museum. I saw them there."

"So, you know everything then. Why are you asking me questions?"

"Well, because you said there's nothing to see," I said, my brain hurting from the way the conversation was going round in circles.

"Nothing to see with our eyes, yes, but we don't see everything with our eyes, do we, boy? We can see things with our brains and our hearts. But if you run around like crazy things you'll see nothing. So, go and climb the tree, but no running, shouting or singing and maybe you'll see something."

The three of us started walking, very quietly, towards the tree, before she said something else.

As we walked the sky darkened again. The cloud was back.

"That was a powerful spell," Bul-Boo said, laughing.

"Well, you can get temporary spells," Madillo replied, "and the cloud is not as dark as it was. I think the storm has been averted."

I didn't say anything as the doom had returned, heavier than ever, and taken over my legs and made them so bendy that I started to feel a bit like a rubber man. Madillo told me once about a character in one of the anime things she watches who eats gum-gum fruit and turns into a rubber man. He's called Monkey-something, and after he's stretched he snaps back into shape just like a rubber band. That was me as I waited to be struck dead.

I was not sure I could make it all the way to the tree and started trying to think of other things that might make my legs return to normal. I stared at the ground and thought about the time we were in Kafue National Park and an elephant chased us because she had her calf with her. She came so close to the car her trunk hit the back window.

It seemed to be working. I was starting to feel less wobbly. I looked up and realized I was completely

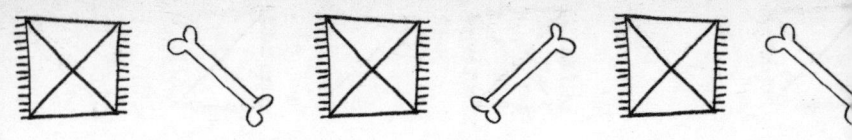

alone at the foot of the tree. Bul-Boo and Madillo had disappeared.

At that moment Rubber Man disappeared altogether and in his place stood Ice Man. Frozen. I couldn't even turn my head to see whether Nokokulu had also gone. I felt as if it was just me, the tree and the wicked souls of Nokokulu's long-lost ancestors.

Suddenly I heard a noise – a rough scraping against the bark above me.

"Fred, why are you just standing there? Come up!"

Bul-Boo. The voice of my dreams in the middle of a waking nightmare.

I looked up slowly, careful not to snap my frozen neck.

There they were. Sitting in a bend of the tree, grinning down at me.

"I'm standing here because I'm enjoying the view," I said in my most casual voice.

"Of the ground?" asked Bul-Boo.

"Yes. There happens to be what looks like a rare praying mantis here. It's got purple stripes on its body."

Silence. For a few satisfying moments.

"Are you sure?" Bul-Boo again, her voice incredulous.

"I'm the one looking at it, aren't I?" I said.

I was on a roll here. Ice Man and Rubber Man had left the building.

"I don't believe you," she said. "I'm coming down to look."

Oh dear. The end of the roll.

"I don't think you'll see it. It's started burrowing into a hole. I don't want to stop it, because it would be terrified and might have a heart attack."

Why didn't I just say it had flown away? Because that's what praying mantises do. They fly. They don't burrow.

"Burrowing?" said Bul-Boo, looking not at me but at Madillo.

"It's a new species," Madillo explained. "Fred has made a major scientific discovery. He'll be hailed the world over for discovering the Purple-striped Burrowing Praying Mantis."

"Well?" Bul-Boo said, after a pause. "Are you coming up?"

I nodded. Not trusting my voice, which seemed to be busy betraying me.

"It's great up here. You can see everything," she told me.

"Except praying mantises," added Madillo.

She never lets anything go.

BUL-BOO

On Top of the Baobab Tree

You'd never be able to climb a baobab if it hadn't fallen over. Well, I wouldn't anyway. The bark feels so smooth and the wrinkles are facing upwards, so you can't put your feet onto anything. On this one the wrinkles were sideways and there were lots of knots. I saw someone once who put little pegs into a baobab so they could climb up it, but you wouldn't need them for this one.

I love being at the top of a tree. And being at the top of a sideways baobab is the same as being at the top of a normal tree. From where we were we could see for ever – the Kariba Dam in the distance and the Zambezi and Lusitu rivers.

Fred came up after his excuse about watching the

praying mantis. I didn't tease him about it. He knows I know he made it up, so there would be no point.

"What's Nokokulu doing?" I asked. We had a good view of her and she was walking around peering at things on the ground.

Fred shrugged. "I don't know. Maybe she's lost something."

"She's a witch," Madillo said. "Witches don't lose things."

"Nokokulu's not a witch," I argued. "I can't believe we're having this conversation again. There's no such thing as witches. It's just pure and undiluted rubbish."

"There's no such thing as pure rubbish. Rubbish can't be pure – that's contradictory," Fred pointed out.

"Depends," I said, not wanting to admit that he was right.

"Depends on nothing," he said indignantly. "Rubbish can't be pure."

I looked away and muttered, "Maybe you're right."

Fred and Madillo didn't say anything. It is rare, I know, for me to admit I'm wrong. That's mainly because I look things up before I say anything, so usually I'm right. But not this time. I must remember to put that in my black notebook: I was wrong today and I admitted it.

"At least this tent zips all the way up, not like the old

one we used when we went to Kundalila Falls," I said to change the subject.

"That was terrible," Madillo agreed. "I kept thinking a crocodile was going to come in through the gap at the front. At least with this one we're safe from anything."

"Plus we don't have to share it with Nokokulu, which is the best part," Fred said. "That would be pretty scary … and loud. Do you know, she says she has never slept in the same room as another human being and she never will?"

"And you believe her?" Madillo said.

"Well … when she was a baby I suppose she had to be in the room with her mother, but she says that from the moment she was born they knew she was special so they gave her her own room."

"She must have shared a room at some point because she gave birth to your granny, who then gave birth to your dad and Aunt Kiki!" Madillo reminded him.

Kiki. Just the name brought it all back. I looked at Fred. He's funny about things that really upset him. He tries very hard not to talk about them. He could talk all day and all night about things like predictions of doom, but when it's something real like Aunt Kiki he just clams up. I saw him wince when Madillo said her name but then he just carried on as normal.

"I know, I know," he said. "But I've never met

my granny. I don't even know if she existed. Maybe Nokokulu is one of those kind of adopted relatives. You know, the ones who come from nowhere."

Madillo looked at me and then at Fred. "You mean like the Adopt a Zebra thing at Munda Wanga? We did that. Dad says we own one of the ears."

Madillo and Fred could fill volumes of notebooks with the ridiculous conversations they have.

"I wonder if the story about Bukoko is true," I said. "It's funny that we've come here just after Sister told us about her."

"We could probably see her grave from here if it was true," Madillo said. "You see over there where those lines of stones are? I think that must have been the graveyard."

Fred and I turned to see what she was pointing at, and there were very neat lines of stones down below in the grass. We had a good view from our high vantage point.

"But we wouldn't find her actual grave, because surely it was dug up along with all the other graves?" I said. "And when they just found a stone in it they probably didn't keep the grave marked."

"Let's take a photo of the stones anyway, to show Sister Leonisa," Madillo suggested. "The actual grave-yard where Bukoko might have been buried."

Sometimes Madillo has really good ideas.

"Do you know," said Fred, as we were starting to climb down the tree. "Because Bukoko was probably a Tonga, her spirit will be here even if her grave isn't."

"What do you mean?" asked Madillo.

Fred grinned. He loves it when he is the only one of us to know something.

"Well, a *muzimu* is a spirit that is left behind when someone dies. And that spirit is then inherited by someone else in the clan. It's a different way of making sure that people live for ever and are never forgotten. So it doesn't matter how many years ago Bukoko died, her spirit will have been inherited, and then when that person died, their spirit will also have been inherited."

Both of us stared at him.

"So," Madillo said slowly, "her spirit could be inside someone who lives in Pambazana, for example, just down the road?"

"Exactly," Fred said.

"And how do you know this, Fred?" I asked him.

"Dad told me about it when I was asking him about reincarnation and Hinduism. He said that although this is different, it's the same idea."

"That means that when I die my *muzimu* will live for ever," Madillo said excitedly, "until there are no more people left on this earth. It's a brilliant idea."

I wasn't quite sure what to think about it as I find

it hard to believe in spirits, but I have to admit that the thought of a little part of me travelling through time is quite nice.

"The downside is that you have no choice in the matter," Fred said. "Your *muzimu* could end up being inherited by anyone. And then you're trapped inside them, being them."

We carried on climbing down the tree, probably all thinking of the person we would least like to end up inside. Then we went over to the stones and spent a long time taking photographs of them. We even moved some of them around to make them look like a little child's grave, which, if I think about it, was a bit morbid. We must have caught that from Sister Leonisa.

By now we had almost forgotten that Nokokulu was somewhere near by and that both Madillo and Fred were feeling doom laden.

Nokokulu reminded us. With a loud blast of her car horn.

"When I grow up I want to be like Nokokulu," Madillo said. "I'll wear whatever I want, and shout if I feel like it, do spells all over the place and be rude to other people's children."

"And drive all over the road?" I asked.

"That too. Did you see how everyone stays out of her way?" Fred said.

"No, Fred," I said. "If you remember we were trapped in the boot."

The blasts of Nokokulu's horn were getting more and more impatient. We couldn't ignore her.

Fred started running towards the car.

"Last one there has to sit in the front seat on the way home!" he shouted. "And it's not going to be me."

FRED

The Cloud of Doom

As I ran towards the car I felt the ground rumbling underneath my feet. Like when you're hungry and your stomach grumbles, only much bigger. The kind of feeling that goes right through your feet to your brain.

"They've opened the Kariba Dam!" I shouted back at Bul-Boo, who was still quite a way behind me.

"What?" Bul-Boo said, slowing down. "Wait – tell me."

I stopped running and waited for her. Forgetting for a minute who I was dealing with – she knows a whole lot more than me about dam walls and the shaking of the earth.

As she reached me she sped up again and ran right past.

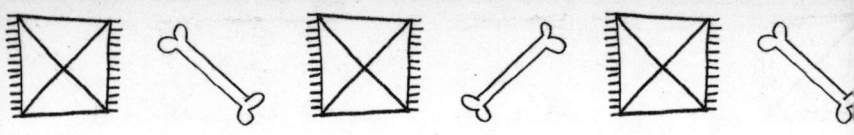

"Sorry, Fred," she called over her shoulder, laughing. "I just don't want to be map reader on the way home."

She reached the car before me but not by much, and she must have forgotten for a moment that Nokokulu was still in it, because as she reached it she banged both her hands on the bonnet and let out a yell. "Back seat for me!"

Not a good move.

"Hey! What did I tell you about noise here? Strange things will happen if you don't listen to your elders, believe me."

My stomach lurched. In my experience my great-granny doesn't make idle threats. When Mum says that she's never cooking us another meal because we just gobble our food and leave, we shake our fingers at her (in a more jokey kind of way than Nokokulu does) and say, "Idle threats!" It makes her mad.

But whatever kind of threat Nokokulu was making, it was a believable one. For me, anyway. Madillo stopped laughing too. Bul-Boo was trying to look as though she had suddenly come upon us entirely by accident and could not believe her bad luck.

"You," Nokokulu said, pointing at her. "Boo! What are you doing?"

"Nothing. I'm doing nothing," Bul-Boo said.

"Well, the storm has gone away and Mad Girl and

Silly Boy aren't going to be any use" – I could tell she had put capital letters in the names by the way she said them – "so you can help me build the fire. You other two, go and play."

As if we were three years old.

"What if the storm comes back?" I asked.

"What if there's a warthog who comes here to eat us all? What if there's a giant snake curled up in the tree and it slithers down in the night? What if the rivers run up the hill and drown us all?" Nokokulu said.

She thinks she's so clever. It's not how ancient people should behave. And I wouldn't mind about the warthog, as I don't think there's a single case in human history of a warthog eating people, but did she have to put the snake in there? Along with the word "slither"?

Bul-Boo smiled at me and I couldn't tell whether it was because of Nokokulu being so rude or the other kind of smile. But I didn't really mind which one it was, either would do.

While Bul-Boo and Nokokulu were setting out the fire (well, Bul-Boo did most of the work: Nokokulu prefers to be the one giving orders), Madillo and I sat a short distance away. Waiting.

I decided to talk to Madillo about the fact that the cloud of doom had not yet gone away from above my head.

"You know my gift?" I said.

I had to say it carefully because all Madillo wants in life is a gift. She thinks it's very unfair that I have one and she doesn't. She keeps trying to create gifts in herself but I've told her you can't do that. You have to be born with them.

She nodded.

"Well, you know I woke up the day before yesterday with a premonition?"

"The doom one?"

"Yes. Like all my others."

"What about it?" she said, tracing circles in the dust with a stick, pretending not to be that interested. I could tell she was desperate to know.

"Well, it's a bad one, and it still hasn't gone away. I can't give you any details, but it means that whatever is going to happen is still ahead of us."

"What's the use of being able to predict bad things if you don't know what they are?" she said. "I could do that and then when something goes wrong, as it always does eventually, I'd say, 'Oh, I knew that was going to happen.'"

I'd never told her that my gift was limited to general awfulness. I'd always just said I didn't want to share the details because they were too depressing. But it looked like she was starting to not believe me.

"It's not like that, Madillo, and this time I'm scared."

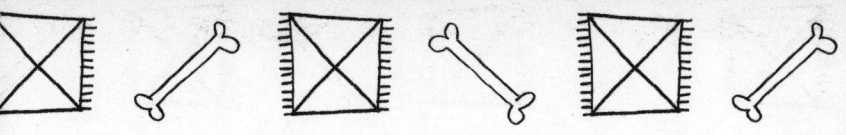

She looked a bit more sympathetic now. "When is this thing going to happen? Do you at least know that?"

"Tonight," I said, before I could stop myself. Even though this wasn't strictly true, I wanted her to think I knew *that* at least.

Madillo went still. "Are you sure?"

I nodded.

"Tonight, here, under the baobab tree where we're surrounded by the bones of dead people? Where we'll be sleeping on top of graves? Where the spirits of Nokokulu's ancestors roam free?"

Bul-Boo always tells me I'm too dramatic about things, but I'm nothing compared to her twin.

"Well, yes," I said defensively.

Why had I said tonight?

"We'll have to tell the others."

"The others plural? You think I'm going to tell Nokokulu? I'm not even going to tell Bul-Boo," I said. "She'll laugh at me."

Madillo looked at me. I could see she was going to say something, but then she didn't.

"OK, you're right. Well, she wouldn't laugh at you, but she wouldn't believe you. I hope you're wrong, Fred. And I hope we get back home soon. We need to carry on the investigation into the disappearance of Aunt Kiki and the others."

I didn't want to say it to Madillo but getting back home was the least of my worries. Nokokulu would get us home even if she took ages about it. It was the thought of Aunt Kiki that was making my head hurt.

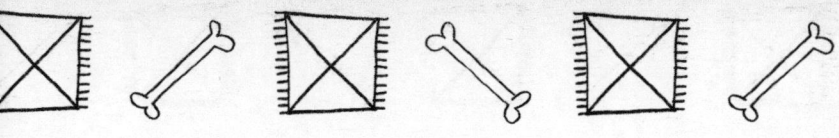

FRED

Nocturnal Lettuce

Nokokulu can be nice when she decides to be, even if it makes her grimace. Today, without me even knowing, she had packed all my favourite foods — sausages, chocolates, baked beans and more chocolates.

"Lucky we have enough for our surprise visitors, Chiti," she said, winking at me.

The raging creature from earlier had clearly disappeared. Maybe it was because she'd had something to eat — half a bar of chocolate while she was watching Bul-Boo do all the work. Bul-Boo says that if people don't eat often enough their blood sugar gets low and it makes them grumpy. That's probably why Nokokulu eats all the time. She must have very sensitive blood sugar.

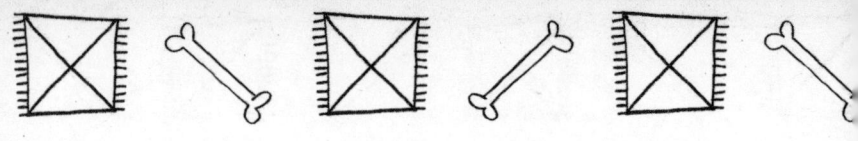

Bul-Boo finished stoking up the fire then came and sat down next to me. Sometimes I wish I didn't like her in the way I think I do, because it makes everything so complicated. We've been friends since we were small and we're just used to each other. I didn't even know now if she was sitting next to me because she liked me or because she was just used to sitting next to me. Last year I wouldn't have thought anything about it.

Nokokulu put her small frying pan carefully onto the coals at the side of the fire so it wasn't in the middle of the flames. She also had a small pot with *nshima* in it and she crouched by the side of the fire, stirring it.

"Good," she said. "Now things are right. We will wait for the food to cook and when we've eaten it all we'll go to bed and give my ancestors some peace."

We all just nodded. Silence is often best when Nokokulu is in a good mood, because it means she stays that way. The sun was starting to go down already so I supposed it would soon be time for bed.

"Yes, boy, it will soon be night," she said, looking at me. (I don't know how she always knows what I'm thinking.) "But who says it has to be dark for you to sleep? Do you think lions look at their watches and wonder if it's too early to go to bed? No, they don't. They sleep in the sun, because that's the best time to sleep."

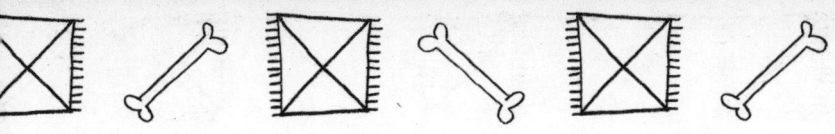

"Lions are nocturnal," Bul-Boo commented.

Bul-Boo knows a lot of interesting facts but I would have preferred her to keep this one to herself.

"Nocturnal?" Nokokulu said. "And you think you aren't?"

Madillo frowned at Bul-Boo to stop her saying anything else. Often it's Bul-Boo trying to get Madillo to be quiet, but today it was the opposite.

"Well, I suppose I could be nocturnal," Bul-Boo said slowly, "if I was a lion."

"And you *could* very easily be one," I jumped in, before World War III started. "We could all be lions. I mean, lions, like humans, are ninety-nine per cent water, so there's very little difference between us."

Bul-Boo turned to look at me. "Fred, are you sure you're not thinking about lettuce?" she asked. "Or jellyfish?"

"Yes," I said, "lettuce. And jellyfish. But they could be nocturnal too if they wanted to be."

There was a small silence following that, which I suppose I should have expected. Because I know there is no such thing as a nocturnal lettuce. I looked across at Nokokulu and she was grinning at me. "Yes, boy, you're right. Anything is possible," she said. "Now, let's eat."

Madillo gave me a thumbs up. Catastrophe avoided. Nokokulu was still in a good mood! Now all I had

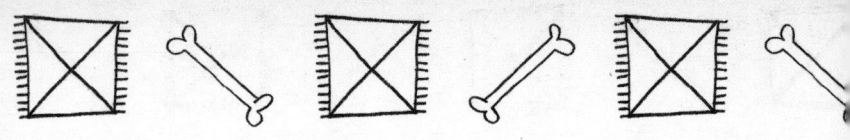

to do was hope that Bul-Boo would try and keep her comments to herself for the rest of the trip.

"You know, children," Nokokulu said as she was dishing food out onto two tin plates, one for her and one for the three of us to share. "A little girl lived here long ago and she flew away from her mother, up into the clouds above us. A small naughty child who never grew, because she wouldn't eat her *nshima*." She didn't look at Bul-Boo when she said that but we all knew who she was talking about. Bul-Boo never eats it. She says that any type of porridge makes her feel ill. I don't understand it but Mum says it's probably just because she likes doing some things that are different from her twin, and Madillo would eat a whole potful of it if you let her.

"Actually," Bul-Boo said (when Bul-Boo uses the word "actually" in that voice, you know she's going to make what she thinks is an important announcement), "the reason that the little girl, who was called Bukoko, didn't grow is because her mother drank too much beer when she was pregnant. It had nothing to do with *nshima*. Sister Leonisa told us about her. Even her name means that."

"Sister Leonisa wouldn't even know how to spell Bukoko," Nokokulu said, raising her eyebrows. "Does she speak ChiTonga? Now, who wants to grow tall and

strong?" she asked, holding out the *nshima* pot.

I nudged Bul-Boo to stop her saying anything else. This time it worked.

BUL-BOO

Old Hidden Face

One thing about Fred that is good and bad all at the same time is that he's quite nosy. He always wants to know what's going on. He had been desperate all day to find out if there was anything in Nokokulu's huge suitcase. When she wandered off after supper for a walk (she says you have to walk after every meal to let your food digest), he sneaked into her tent to take a look. He should have known that the minute he did that, she'd appear. She has a knack of doing that.

When she found him I could hear every word she said. "Nosy, nosy boy!" she shouted. "Trying to look into poor old Nokokulu's suitcase. What are you looking for? You should be careful, you might find something in there that would make you run for a thousand miles.

You would run till those skinny legs of yours could run no more, then you'd fall down into Kalulu the Hare's burrow and that would be the last we'd see of you. Kalulu, you know, is a very tricky hare, and he doesn't like children coming down to disturb him when he's taking a rest."

Fred must have then said something ridiculous, like he was unpacking her suitcase. I couldn't hear him properly.

"How long you think we are staying here? One month? Did you want to put my unpacked clothes in the tent cupboard?" said Nokokulu, clearly warming to her theme. "Where is the tent cupboard? I can't see it. Or maybe you were going to throw my things on the floor?"

There was no answer from Fred.

"Ha!" she said. "One day when you stick your long nose into places it shouldn't be, a big axe will come from nowhere and chop it off. Then what? Then you'll keep it in its proper place. Now go. Leave my things alone."

Fred scuttled out of the tent and back to the fire.

"I don't know what I did to deserve Nokokulu," he said. "If karma is true, she'll come back as a male praying mantis."

"That's not a nice thing to wish on your great-granny, Fred," I said, laughing.

Fred always feels sorry for the male praying mantis

because when it's finished mating it gets its head bitten off by the female. Which really isn't very nice. Fred says it's a female conspiracy and that there are never any fathers around to warn their sons about it because all the fathers are already dead.

"I don't really want her head bitten off, but why does she say all those things to me?" Fred said. "And in front of you and Madillo?"

I couldn't answer that so I changed the subject. "Speaking of heads, do you remember the story Sister told us about that research being done on the guillotine?"

He nodded.

"That scientist who was trying to work out whether people who had their heads chopped off felt any pain? So he asked one man to wink if he was feeling sore once his head was off. And he winked thirteen times. Can you imagine that? A head winking at you as it lay on the ground!"

"And Sister trying to demonstrate by lying on her desk and winking at us. That was funny," Fred said.

"It wasn't funny, it was awful," I told him. "Anyway, did you find out what was in her suitcase?"

"No," he said gloomily. "It was locked and I was just trying to pull one of the sides open so I could look inside when she arrived. You heard the rest."

Singing was coming from the tent. *"Come back here, Chiti, before your nose isn't pretty."*

"That's not normal behaviour," I said.

"Normal?" Fred replied. "That's perfectly normal for her. She makes her own normal."

"We'd better go to her then. Where's Madillo?"

I looked round and saw Madillo crouching down and peering at something on the ground. As we ran to her she stood up.

"Paw prints," she said, pointing.

We both looked down and there they were.

Hyena prints. I knew because of the shape and the toenails.

But only two?

I knew Fred and I would be thinking the same thing. Kryptops. The one Sister Leonisa calls the Old Hidden Face because most of the monster's face was hidden

underneath bumpy horny skin. David in our class secretly calls Sister "Kryptops" but I think that's a bit mean.

OK, so a kryptops' paw prints would have been bigger than these, but I'd never seen such huge hyena prints.

I broke the silence. "These weren't here earlier."

"I know." Fred looked positively ill.

"I thought lions wouldn't come this close, because of the village near by?" Madillo said.

"*Hyenas*, Madillo. Don't you remember those prints Dad showed us in Luangwa? With the pointy toenails?"

"Well, lion, hyena, what's the difference? Both of them could eat us and I don't think they'd be particularly worried if we got them muddled up. Do you think they'd pause between mouthfuls to ask, 'Did you really get me confused with a lion?' Sometimes you're just too particular, Bul-Boo."

I wasn't going to reply to that.

"Do you see there are only two paw prints?" Fred said.

Madillo knelt down next to them. "You're right. Only two."

"There's something very strange going on," Fred said. "I don't like it." He paused and then whispered, "What if it's the Man-Beast?"

"The Man-Beast is something Nokokulu made up," I said, trying to sound as though I believed what I was

saying. "There's probably a really simple explanation. The poor hyena must have been walking along minding its own business and the wind came up and blew away the prints. But these two weren't blown away, because they were protected."

"By what?"

"Well, by this rock," I said, pointing to something that couldn't really be called a rock. More like a small stone.

"You mean this pebble?" Madillo said.

I must write down Madillo's sole purpose in life in my notebook: Never Let Bul-Boo Get Away With Anything At All.

"This pebble could change the course of a hurricane. Geology is a complex thing," I said, hoping that would end the conversation.

At that moment a small shadow fell across the paw prints. Nokokulu had arrived.

She looked down at the ground and said nothing, which was unusual for her. Suddenly she didn't look like her usual bossy rude self. She looked scared.

"Did you make these?" she said finally, looking at the three of us.

We all shook our heads.

She crouched down next to them and looked up at us again. "Are you sure?"

"We didn't, Nokokulu," Fred said. "But why are there only two?"

"Ha!"

Sometimes when she says "Ha!" she sounds triumphant, as if she has just reached the top of Mount Kilimanjaro carrying three cheetahs on her back. But this "Ha!" had an "I told you so" sound to it.

"How many paw prints do you want?" she said, grinning at Fred as if she'd just said something really clever.

"I don't want any prints, Nokokulu, but I don't understand why there are only two."

"Why do you need to understand everything, boy? Two feet, three feet, four feet, why is there a problem? Maybe its other feet were bitten off by a lion, so now it has to walk on two? A sad two-legged hyena. Don't be thinking about them any more. Leave these silly things and come and help me put out the fire so we can go to sleep."

We left the paw prints reluctantly and followed her back to the fire.

I couldn't shake the feeling that there was something she was not telling us. Something she knew about the prints. Anyone looking at them would see they were real, so why had she asked us if we had made them? It was almost as if she didn't want them to be.

She stopped when we got near the fire. "You two,"

she said, pointing at Fred and me, "you get some sand to put out the fire."

"And me?" asked Madillo.

"You…" Nokokulu thought for a minute. "You can go back to those silly hyena prints and cover them over with sand. Then they're gone. If a hyena can't see his own prints he won't come back to that place."

"What?" I said, confused.

"Come on," she said, ignoring me. "Run along now, Mad Girl."

Madillo didn't wait for a second instruction.

I know that it's not true about a hyena's paw prints. If it was true it would mean that a hyena would never go anywhere new. In fact it would never even have taken its first steps, as it would have looked up at its hyena mother and said, "I can't move, because none of my paw prints are on this earth."

Then it would have just stood completely still till it died.

But there was no point telling Nokokulu that.

After we'd put out the fire and Madillo had come back, Nokokulu said, "Don't be frightened tonight. The Cow Who Lies Down is watching over us, and the two-legged hyena has gone for ever … if his paw prints have been fully erased."

A simple goodnight would have done me.

"And I'm right here in the next tent if anything happens."

"As if that's going to make us feel any better," Madillo said under her breath. She still hasn't learnt that Nokokulu is The One Who Sees All and Hears All.

"Ha!" Nokokulu said as she crawled into her tent and zipped it up.

We all went into our tent but we left the flap open as it was still quite warm. The sun had gone down but the night air wasn't cool yet.

"We can't stay in here all night," I whispered. "We'll melt."

What I meant was that I couldn't bear the thought of lying awake in the tent worrying about those prints. And remembering Nokokulu's face when she first saw them.

"We could wait till she's asleep then go outside and play *nsolo*?" Fred said hopefully.

"We won't have to wait long," Madillo replied. "Listen. She's started again."

She was right. The rumbling snores could be heard once more.

Fred looked at us expectantly. "So?"

Madillo and I looked at one another.

"Is it safe?" Madillo asked.

"You mean from the hyena?" I said.

She nodded.

"We'll be sitting right outside the tent flap and if we hear anything we'll jump back in," Fred said.

Fred loves *nsolo*. He forgets all his worries once he starts playing it.

"Well, OK," I said. "You dig the holes and we'll get the stones. We can use my torch."

"But," Madillo said, "no shouting. It will have to be a silent game, OK?"

Fred and I nodded. It is almost impossible to play *nsolo* silently, but I reckoned the thought of Nokokulu waking up and finding us outside the tent would keep us quiet.

We played for what seemed like ages – and the whole time I felt as if there was someone watching me. But there was no one. Madillo was not her usual self, even though she was trying hard to be. I don't think either of us felt like playing, but it was better than just lying in the tent wondering. Fred didn't seem too worried, especially as he kept winning. His doom feeling seemed to be forgotten for now. I reckon he could have carried on playing all night.

The night was very still, so once the cicadas stopped their singing all was quiet apart from the steady rumble of Nokokulu's snores. We had set up the torch on a stone and it made strange shadows across the game.

I was relieved when Madillo said, "I'm tired now, Fred."

"Tired of losing?" Fred asked.

"No, just tired," she whispered. "And I think Nokokulu might be waking up."

We listened. The snores had stopped. That was enough to persuade Fred, so we all crawled back into our tent.

BUL - BOO

Fred's Laughing Hyena

When we got back inside the tent we zipped up the flap. I didn't mind how warm the night was, I wasn't going to sleep with the flaps open. We then laid out Fred's sleeping bag on the floor and used our jackets as pillows. Fred lay down between us. He's always the one in the middle.

"It's funny to think we're lying on ground that all those ancient people lived and died on," Madillo whispered once we were all settled.

"It is," I said. "I suppose we're always on ground that ancient people lived and died on, but it seems more strange now, being here. Especially thinking about Bukoko running about on this very spot on her little legs."

"I keep thinking about those paw prints," Fred said. "I have never, ever seen only two prints like that. It's

weird. I wish we'd taken a photo of them. Maybe that would have been better than just wiping them away. I remember Sister saying that photographs steal your soul or something."

"Not a hyena's soul," I told him, wishing he hadn't raised it again. "What she said was that in some cultures people used to believe that if you had your photo taken your soul would be stolen and imprisoned in the picture. *She* doesn't believe that. And it's not something I've heard of in relation to animals."

"It's all right, anyway," Fred said, "because the prints aren't there now."

There was a silence in the tent, and if it's possible to be especially silent that's what Madillo was being.

"Aren't they, Madillo?" Fred said finally.

A few seconds later she spoke, and her voice was thin and quiet.

"I didn't wipe them away."

"I knew it!" Fred sat up and banged his head on the tent pole.

Madillo didn't answer.

"Why, Madillo?" I exclaimed.

"I don't know! I went back to the spot and I was going to kick sand over them but then I couldn't. I don't know why." She sounded upset.

"They will have blown away by now anyway," I said

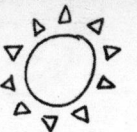

quickly to reassure her, "and that thing about hyenas never coming back to a place if they can't see their own paw prints is just something Nokokulu made up." Madillo should have told us she hadn't wiped the paw prints away but I hate it when she's sad.

"But if she said we must wipe away the prints then she must know something," Fred pointed out. "Something we don't know. I know you don't believe in her having powers, Bul-Boo, but you've never proved scientifically that she doesn't."

"That's like saying you can't prove that the Flying Spaghetti Monster is not real, so therefore it probably is," I said. "Science is not for proving that mad things are just made up. That's just wasting Science's time. Even the people who created the Flying Spaghetti Monster admit that they did. So why would you drag Science out to prove it?"

"Science isn't a person. You can't waste Science's time," Fred said. "And do you remember that story about how Nokokulu made a man grow goat's horns on his head? How would you explain that?"

"The difference is that we never saw it, did we? She told us she'd done it. She could have been making it up. Like she is about the hyena prints," I added.

"But," Madillo interrupted, still in her small voice, "I should have wiped them away. Even if there is

0.0001 per cent chance that Nokokulu's not making it up, I still should have wiped them away. I don't know why I didn't. It was as if my feet were paralysed – I couldn't kick the sand over them. I'll have to go back there and do it."

Fred and I went silent for a few seconds.

"Madillo," I said eventually, "you don't have to. It was just Nokokulu being Nokokulu. She likes seeing the scared look on our faces, that's all."

Madillo didn't answer.

"I'm not sure," Fred said. "That would just be mean, and she's not really mean. Well, not often. It could be true, you never know. It could be an old hyena who's forgetful, like Nokokulu is herself."

I wished for one moment that I was a witch and I could cast a spell of silence over Fred. With every word he spoke Madillo's face looked more worried. She was twisting her hair round and round with her finger, which is what she does when she's anxious.

"What if it's true?" she whispered. "What if the two-legged hyena comes back here? Anything could happen, anything at all. I have to go and wipe those prints away." She looked at me and her voice came back. "I have to, Bul-Boo. We have no other choice."

I felt my heart sink. When Madillo gets that look on her face it would take an earthquake to change her mind.

"There's no such thing as a two-legged hyena," I said. "You know that the kryptops died out millions of years ago. And even if there was such a thing and it happened to be here, it's dark and you don't have any shoes on and I know there are scorpions out there." Which was a bit of a low blow as Madillo hates scorpions.

She turned away, reaching for her shoes. "Shoes are easy to put on, Bul-Boo. I don't care what you say. I'm going to wipe those paw prints away and there's nothing you can do to stop me. I won't sleep if I don't." She stood up. "I'm taking the torch. I won't even be gone a minute. You two will be OK in the dark for that long—"

"But if you have the torch then the hyena will be able to see you," an unsilent Fred interrupted.

"Fred!"

"A torch won't make a difference," said Madillo. "Hyenas have acute hearing and sense of smell, and they have night vision. A torch won't make a difference. If it's around, it will know I'm there, torch or no torch."

"Madillo, don't be silly," I pleaded. "It's late. We can do it in the morning."

The minute those words were out of my mouth, I knew I had lost the battle. Madillo can't stand it when I call her silly.

She raised her eyebrows. "Silly? I don't think so. This is my business. I'll sort it out. And you're not always

right, Bul-Boo. Sometimes you have to let me make my own decisions."

I hate it when she gets like this. Dad says she's as stubborn as a block of wood, and right now that's exactly what she was.

"Listen," I said, hoping to distract her. "We've been here for ages now. Have either of you heard anything that even vaguely resembles a hyena? No. There isn't one out there."

Fred suddenly started laughing in a high-pitched hyena-like way and Madillo and I both jumped. Sometimes he drives me mad.

Madillo looked at him and unzipped the tent. "That's not funny," she said. "I'm going to do this and then I'll be back." She hesitated. "If I'm not back in a few minutes come and find me."

With that she stepped outside.

Fred looked at me. I shrugged my shoulders – I knew there was nothing I could do. When Madillo decides something, that's it. A bit like me. Which is not surprising, I suppose. I could follow her but she'd be looking over her shoulder and then she'd get cross and Nokokulu would wake up and we'd all be in trouble.

There wasn't any such thing as a two-legged hyena anyway, so there was nothing to worry about.

MADILLO

Moon Shadow

Each step that took me away from the tent felt like a mile. I don't know why I hadn't asked the others to come with me. I would have felt better with them right next to me. The moon seemed to be creeping in and out of the clouds as if it was following me. I wished I had wiped the paw prints away when the sun was still out.

If I get scared at night-time, I always think about tomorrow. Tomorrow it will be morning; the sun will be shining. I'll wake up and I'll be talking to Bul-Boo and Fred. We'll make breakfast from the leftover food and it will all be normal.

I was nearly at the paw prints but it felt as if I had been walking for hours. The moment I reached them

the moon came out from behind the clouds, almost as if it was showing me where they were. Somehow they looked bigger than before and as I stepped closer I thought I heard something like loud breathing, in and out, in and out. I listened. It stopped.

I took another step and the breathing started again. Slow breaths, in and out, in and out. I turned my head but could see nothing. Only the moon and the clouds. The sound stopped and all I could hear was the high-pitched buzz of the cicadas.

I stepped forward again, ready to run if the breathing sound returned, and a shadow fell over the prints. I looked up at the sky but at that moment the clouds crossed the moon and it went completely dark. I felt cold suddenly. The kind of cold that takes over your whole body. My legs started shaking and I felt myself falling. As if in a dream. Falling, falling with nothing to stop me.

FRED

Silent Echoes

"Bul-Boo," I said.

"Yes?"

"We shouldn't have let her go on her own."

"She's very stubborn. She wouldn't have let us come with her. Anyway, it's very close. We'd hear if anything happened to her."

How was that supposed to be comforting? So, if Madillo's bones were being crunched up, we'd hear? And then what would we do?

I shone my torch across at Bul-Boo. She was lying perfectly still and her eyes were closed.

"Are you going to sleep?" I asked.

"We always know when the other one is all right. It doesn't matter where we are. She will be fine. If there

179

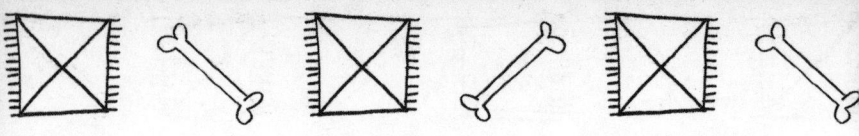

was something wrong I'd know. That's how identical twins are."

"That doesn't always work," I argued.

"It's worked so far," she said, her voice cracking a little.

The tent went silent again. I kept waiting for the sound of returning footsteps but heard nothing.

Finally Bul-Boo spoke. "It's been two minutes. Should we wait a bit longer or should we go out and look?"

"I don't know."

We waited.

"Three minutes."

I think this was only the second time I had ever heard Bul-Boo sound scared, and she wasn't even trying to disguise it.

"Let's go," I said.

We both jumped up, put our shoes on and crawled out of the tent.

The air felt clammy and warm against my skin as I stood up and looked around. It was dark and very, very still.

Bul-Boo reached out and grabbed my hand. "Fred, I can't hear anything. Listen."

We stopped moving. She was right. The air seemed empty of sounds. No cicadas buzzing. No nightjars. No snores.

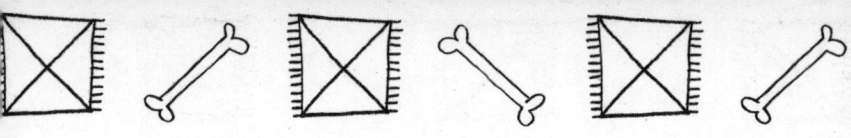

"There's something wrong," she said, her voice a shaky whisper. "The night is never this quiet."

"Let's call her," I said.

We both shouted at the same time, "Madillo ... Madillo!"

Our voices sounded loud in the night, echoing into the silence.

We stood and waited.

Nothing. Silence again, apart from Bul-Boo's breathing, which seemed to be getting louder every second.

"Madillo!" she shouted. "Where are you? Stop hiding – it's not funny."

Silence.

Then we heard a loud noise from Nokokulu's tent and both jumped.

She crawled out and stood up. "Noise, noise, in the middle of the night. What are you doing?" she shouted.

"Nokokulu!" Bul-Boo said, tears rolling down her cheeks. "Madillo's gone."

"Gone where?"

"I don't know. She went to clean away the hyena's footprints, because she ... forgot to do it earlier. She said she would be quick, but she hasn't come back. We called her."

Nokokulu stared at Bul-Boo. "When did she go?"

"Five minutes ago."

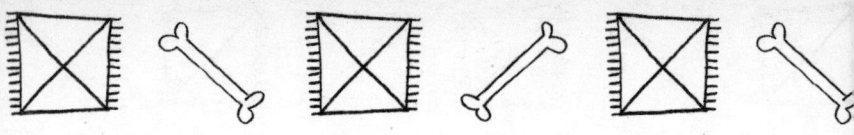

"You, Chiti, you didn't go with her? You let her go outside into the night on her own?"

"Yes, Nokokulu," I replied, not looking at her.

"Nooo!" whispered Nokokulu to herself. "This was not how it was supposed to be. They were not meant to be here. She was not meant..." She stopped.

Bul-Boo grabbed my arm and started shaking it. She was sobbing loudly now. "I don't understand," she said. "What's happening? What is Nokokulu talking about?"

Nokokulu took hold of Bul-Boo's other hand. "Don't worry, little girl, I know what to do. We'll find her."

With that she disappeared back into the tent, leaving me and Bul-Boo outside staring at one another.

"What's she saying?" Bul-Boo asked me. "Where's Madillo?"

She was still crying. I felt sick in my stomach, as if someone had punched me hard. I didn't know what to do.

"I'll go and look," I said. "Wait here."

I left her there outside Nokokulu's tent and started walking towards where the prints had been. I had never felt more afraid in my life, or more alone.

My eyes had got used to the darkness by now but it didn't make it any better. There seemed to be shadows appearing and disappearing and I felt a small cold wind

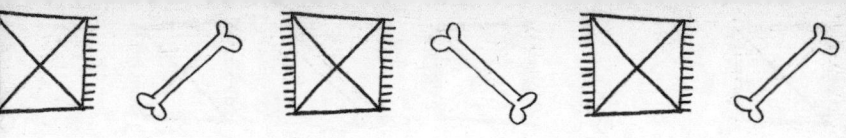

on my face even though it was such a hot night.

I began to walk faster and started calling Madillo's name over and over again, my voice floating uselessly in the air. She wasn't going to answer, I knew that. Each time I said her name it caught in my throat.

When I got nearer to where we'd found the paw prints I slowed down, looking at the ground as I walked. But all I found when I reached the spot was dust and dirt scattered all over the place. No paw prints. And no footprints. Just mad patterns in the sand, like a person with huge hands had sat down and played in it, spreading everything this way and that.

I didn't want this to be happening.

"MADILLO!" I shouted at the top of my voice. "Madillo, can you hear me?"

I heard something. It sounded like a voice, a very faint voice. I felt a little tingle run down my arms.

"Madillo! Madillo!" I called again, sure now that she could hear me.

I listened. The voice came back, quieter.

Then nothing. Dark, deep silence.

FRED

The Call of the Nightjar

I stood there making promises to myself: if Madillo comes back safely I will never be horrible to Joseph again; I will stop making up stories about Nokokulu; I will tidy my room once a week and never, ever complain about anything that is put on my plate. I'll do anything. Anything.

The moon suddenly came out from behind the clouds, and it felt almost as bright as daylight. Now I could see everything around me: the car in the distance, the tents next to the Sleeping Cow tree and Bul-Boo standing completely still where I had left her.

I panicked at the suddenness of the moonlight, like a torch shining down from the sky, and began to run back to the tents.

Bul-Boo didn't move. She looked almost like a statue, as if she was afraid to move even one muscle.

I stopped in front of her.

"I think I heard something, Bul-Boo, a voice. It sounded like Madillo."

"Are you sure?" she asked, her voice catching in her throat. "Where did you hear it? Is she close? Let's go, Fred. Come on."

I wished I hadn't said it: I didn't even know if it was a voice. It could have been an owl. I can never seem to stop myself exaggerating, even when it's a situation as bad as this was.

"Wait," Nokokulu called from inside the tent. "Don't go anywhere. Stay there, I'm coming out."

She sounded different somehow. Her voice was deeper than usual. It was as if someone else was speaking through her mouth.

We waited.

Inside the tent she was obviously moving about. We heard rustling and clinking, then deep mumbling words that I couldn't understand.

We waited some more. Bul-Boo's fingers were hurting my arm she was holding it so tightly.

"Please, Nokokulu," Bul-Boo said, her voice shaking. "Please come out now."

The tent unzipped and Nokokulu appeared. She

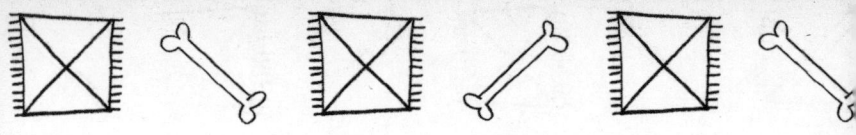

looked at Bul-Boo and a different tone came into her voice. It was almost kind.

"I know. I know what you are thinking, little girl, but don't think that. We'll find your sister. I will find your sister."

"But the hyena…" Bul-Boo began. "And Fred heard a voice answering him."

"It wasn't a voice. It was his own voice echoing off the waters of the Kariba Dam, fooling you into thinking that. The river never wanted to be a dam and it mocks us if we make sounds around it. Did it sound like a girl, Chiti?"

"I don't know." I had never felt more miserable in my whole life.

Nokokulu stamped her foot. "Don't say anything if you don't know, boy. Now, you two have to do exactly what I tell you. I don't want arguments," she added, looking straight at Bul-Boo. "You understand me?"

Neither of us answered.

"I will find your sister and I will bring her back to you. I want you to stay here, both of you. You are to light the fire and pack away the tents. I have packed my suitcase and locked it. You, Chiti, must put the suitcase, the tents and everything else into the car. But do not wait in the car. Wait here next to the fire. If you talk, then you must talk very quietly. Can you do this?"

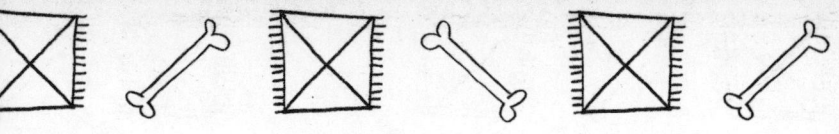

"But Nokokulu…" Bul-Boo said.

"But nothing, child. You must do what I say and do it properly."

"Why can't we come and help you?" I asked.

"I don't need help, especially from you. Was it me who let the little mad one go out on her own in the night to where the hyena had been?"

The kind tone in her voice had disappeared very fast.

That was the end of the conversation. Nokokulu, with no torch or stick or anything, walked off. I watched her and suddenly she seemed to me to be just a tiny old lady hobbling away, an old lady with no powers whatsoever. How could *she* find Madillo?

Bul-Boo and I started taking the tents down without speaking. All you could hear was the rustling of the tent material and our breathing. We carried everything to the car then locked it.

Bul-Boo lit the fire again and it burned bright against the dark sky. I sat down and she came to sit beside me. It's funny how things happen. I'd been wanting her to sit next to me, to hold my hand, to do anything that showed that she liked me – and now she was, and now I didn't care, because all I could think about was Madillo. I could feel Bul-Boo beside me. She'd gone so sad she'd stopped saying anything. It was like her words were trapped inside her. I felt like a

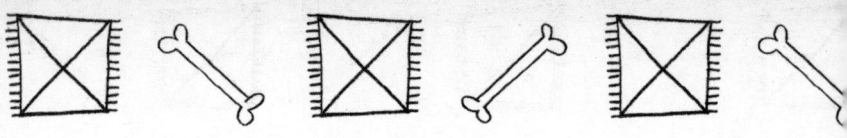

useless clumsy thing sitting next to her.

It was all my fault this had happened. I knew something was going to. I knew it from the moment I woke up on Thursday morning. I knew it all day yesterday and all day today. But still I let Madillo leave our tent and go out by herself into the night. If she'd been taken away by the hyena I might as well have murdered her. If that was the case, I didn't want to be alive, because it would live with me for the rest of my life. Every morning when I woke up, even before I opened my eyes, the first thing I'd think would be that I'd killed her.

And the worst part of it was that the cloud of doom that had been over my head was now gone. It had just vanished. Which could only mean one thing – the worst possible thing had happened.

When I was very small I used to cry a lot, if I fell out of a tree or banged my head. Stupid sore things. And I didn't mind who saw me or heard me. Mum said I cried louder than anyone she'd ever met. But I'd not cried for a very long time. I think since I was ten.

And now I couldn't help it.

I was sitting there with Bul-Boo, staring into the fire feeling as if my head was going to explode, and it started. Big stinging tears rolled down my face and there was nothing I could do. I could feel Bul-Boo turn her head to look at me and then her hand got hold of mine

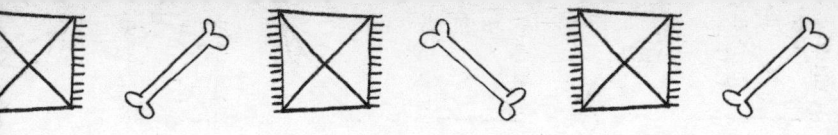

and we just sat there, the two of us crying and crying. It felt like we would never be able to stop.

I kept putting more wood onto the fire just so I would have something to do. Just so I'd feel useful.

Every time we heard a sound we'd both jump. I knew there couldn't be snakes because they don't like fire, but some of the noises came from the tree, almost like something was running around on the trunk. Sometimes I heard the sound of a nightjar. Dad told me once that the noise they make is called churring, and it sounds like that – like a long drawn out *churrrrrrrrrrrrrrrr*. It would have been a nice sound to hear if we had just been in the garden back home. But not there. There the only sound I wanted to hear was the sound of Madillo's voice.

BUL-BOO

Shadows Short, Shadows Tall

No time ever passed as slowly as that night. I felt as if Fred and I had been sitting there for our whole lives. As if days had passed since we'd watched Madillo crawling out of the tent. Hours since Nokokulu had walked off into the night. Now it was just us – me and Fred alone in the shadow of the sleeping baobab tree. I couldn't even phone Mum and Dad because I wouldn't be able to find any words to say to them. And they were so far away. I tried thinking about anything else, about the investigation into Aunt Kiki's disappearance, but I couldn't. Nothing else seemed to matter now.

Fred kept trying to talk to me, but the only person I wanted to talk to was Madillo and she wasn't here.

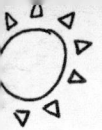

I didn't know where she was. I didn't know anything any more.

The moon had got brighter and brighter as the hours passed and the clouds all disappeared, but I didn't care about that. I just felt like an empty person, as if there was a huge hole in me where I used to be.

Fred started confessing something to me and even though I heard some of the words, nothing much made any sense. He was trying to say it was his fault because he had known something bad was going to happen, he had known since yesterday or the day before. I didn't want him to talk about it: I didn't care whose fault it was. I just wanted Madillo back. Nothing else.

Suddenly I felt it. Something was moving.

I held onto Fred's hand as tightly as I could. "I can feel something," I whispered. "Can you?"

"No, what?"

"Someone is near by. I can feel it."

I felt the hairs on the back of my neck stand up and a shiver go through me.

"Fred," I said, "look."

Two human-shaped shadows stretched out from behind the tree. They were moving. A long one and a very short one.

My heart sounded like a drum beat in my head. I felt as though I wouldn't be able to stand up. And then

I heard a scream, but it was my own.

I couldn't stop. It was as if I had no control over my voice, screaming out into the night.

Then suddenly I heard a familiar "Aiyeee!"

That stopped me. It was Nokokulu.

Fred and I jumped up from the fireside. "Nokokulu."

The shorter, Nokokulu-shaped shadow came out from behind the tree.

She was alone.

"Where is she? Where's Madillo?" I shouted.

"She's all right," Nokokulu said. "Nothing's wrong. She's just asleep."

I didn't answer. I just ran past her to behind the tree. Then I stopped as I saw a tall thin man walking slowly towards me. He was carrying a bundle, and as the moon shone down on it I could see Madillo's curly brown hair. I stood still, my legs as heavy as concrete.

The man carried on walking. Slowly and carefully.

He stopped when he reached me.

"She will be well now," he said, bending down so that Madillo's head was next to mine. "She will be well."

His voice sounded like the molasses they feed the cattle, thick and sweet. It made me feel as if I was about to fall asleep standing there in front of him. I could do nothing, only nod my head.

Madillo was fast asleep, in the deepest sleep I had ever seen. Even her eyelids were still.

I looked at her and found my voice again. "But she doesn't sleep like that. She wakes up so quickly if there's noise. Why isn't she waking up?"

"She is the same like you, I know that. Same face, same thinking. I know you are scared, but you mustn't be. She needs to sleep now. You must be patient."

He stood up and smiled. "Patience, that is all."

I nodded.

"So," Nokokulu muttered, "you don't even know his name and you nod your head like a small wagtail bird. But me you don't believe. Me, who has known you since you were the size of baby warthogs. Ha!" She pointed to the tall man. "You," she said, "come with us to the car and put the child inside. We are leaving."

The man didn't seem to mind how she spoke to him. He just bowed his head and began walking towards the car. He looked as though he was moving very slowly, but his footsteps were so big that we had to run to keep up with him. He was taller than anyone I had ever met and his neck was as long and thin as a piece of bamboo. I don't know how it held his head up. He was wearing loose baggy shorts, and around each ankle were bracelets that looked like they were made of copper, glinting in the moonlight.

I grabbed onto the back of his shirt as he walked, to make sure he didn't disappear with Madillo. Fred sprinted ahead of us to unlock the car door. The tall man leant down and gently laid Madillo on the back seat. I jumped in afterwards and curled up next to her holding her hands, which felt very cold.

I looked up at the man. "When will she wake up?" I asked. "Her hands are so cold. Is she all right? Are you sure she's all right?" I had started crying again. She looked so small and weak and she wasn't moving.

The man gave me a gentle smile. "She's very tired, so she'll sleep for a long time, but it will be all right. In the morning she will wake up." He looked at me. "She will wake up, I promise you."

I believed him.

FRED

An Alive Something

Nokokulu had got into the car and she started the engine while I was still standing there, so I jumped into the passenger seat, and without another word to the tall man she drove off.

I looked out of my window and saw him running back into the bush. I don't know if it was because of his long neck, but he ran like a giraffe. You never notice how fast giraffes run as they take such long steps. I didn't know why the tall man was running, but I didn't feel like asking Nokokulu when she was driving. She'd turn to look at me when she answered and forget to look at the road.

Suddenly something bumped into my side of the car and I heard a soft thud, as if we'd gone into a sandbank

or something. Or hit an animal. Or maybe a human. I was in the car with Mum one day when a dog ran into the road and we knocked into him. It felt like that.

"Aiyeee!" Nokokulu yelled as she slammed on the brakes. (That was the second time she'd said that tonight. I honestly preferred "Ha!" – her "Aiyeee" is high-pitched and goes right through your head.)

I looked into the back seat and saw that now Bul-Boo was fast asleep too. She and Madillo were lying almost in a heap on top of one another, a tangle of twins.

"I'll go and look, Nokokulu," I said, "but keep the lights on."

I didn't especially feel like getting out of the car but thought I'd try to be the brave one.

"You stay in the car," she instructed. "It doesn't matter what it is. The car's all right – we can carry on driving."

I don't know anyone else on this earth who would say something like that. There could be a person lying half dead in the road and Nokokulu was happy to leave them there as long as her car was OK.

"But…"

"How many times must I tell you, I don't want to hear you say 'but'? It's the most foolish word in the dictionary. If I was in charge I would take the word out of

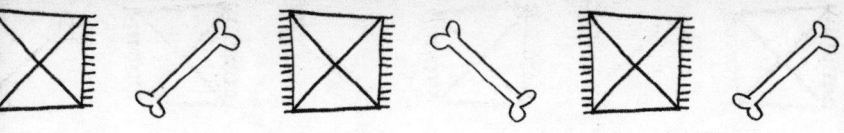

every dictionary and hang it up in the street so people could laugh at it."

She started the car and began to move off.

I turned round and stretched up to look out of the back window.

By the light of the moon I could see a large shape, almost as big as a lion, lying on the road. As I stared at it I swear I saw it lift its head weakly and stare back at me with small shining eyes. Then it flopped down again as if it was dead.

I sat back down quickly in my seat and turned to Nokokulu. She was looking straight ahead as if nothing had happened.

"There was something on the road, Nokokulu," I said.

"What kind of something?"

"I don't know, but I think it was alive. It was looking at me."

"Ha! An alive something looking at you. Chiti, one day you will make up a story that someone will believe and then you'll be in real trouble. Find the map so we can get home."

Home was the only place I wanted to be right now, and as far away as I could ever get from the creature lying on the ground behind us, so I took out the map and started reading.

For once in her life Nokokulu followed my instructions and we went straight home, no detours or stops or anything. There was not a single sound from the back seat the whole way. Both Madillo and Bul-Boo slept even when the sun started to rise. Nokokulu didn't have much to say either, so the only voice in the car was mine telling her when to turn and when to go straight on.

As we came nearer to Lusaka I turned to her and asked, "Nokokulu, what are you going to tell Mum and Dad?"

I think it was the wrong thing to say.

"What?"

That was not the Kind Voice.

"Well … we're arriving back so early and the twins are sleeping and…" I suddenly remembered. "They don't even know we have the twins with us."

"So?" she said.

"So what will you tell them?"

"I don't have to tell them anything, boy. You tell them the truth. The truth is sometimes a good thing."

That would have been fine if it was a normal adult saying it, but in Nokokulu's case I don't think she'd know the truth if it walked up to her on a sunny day and said, "Pleased to meet you. Call me Truth."

So I asked her, "What truth?"

"That we went on a nice holiday to Ng'ombe Ilede, and we set up our tents by the side of the great tree, we spoke to my ancestors and I told you nice stories. We decided to come back early because we were hungry. That truth. You have another truth you want to tell them, boy?"

Another one? "No, Nokokulu, that truth is OK."

"And the *mpundu* – we send them home before your mum and dad wake up and everything will be all right."

So she said.

BUL-BOO

Aunt Kiki and the Snake Oil Salesmen

We were approaching Lusaka when I woke. I could see the orange glow of the city ahead of us. I looked down at Madillo. She was still fast asleep. But now it looked like a more normal sleep. I moved her along the seat so she was more comfortable.

I sat back and closed my eyes. The events of the night didn't seem real. A picture of the tall man who had carried Madillo came into my mind, the way he'd loped across the land and then disappeared from view. I could remember his face so clearly. But perhaps none of it was real. Perhaps Nokokulu had created a shared illusion, a small spell that had caught the three of us in its tentacles. No. Now I was sounding like Madillo – an illusion with tentacles?

I wouldn't think about it. I needed to put the night out of my mind. There were other things I had to be doing. I'd go back to the investigation into Aunt Kiki's disappearance and start by looking at the Holistic Healing Hope website I'd saved to my favourites. It loaded quickly on my phone this time. I followed the **HOPE IN AFRICA!** link. And there it was. A picture of a bright modern building. The caption beneath it said: *Holistic Healing for Zambia.* Ratsberg and Wrath were photographed at the door. Beneath the picture the text said:

> *We have run a clinical trial here in Lusaka. We took eight long-term "AIDS victims". For years they had been forced to take poisonous medicines by ruthless doctors who work for large international drug companies. After three months on our special tablets containing only vitamins and herbs, these people are cured. To order our tablets, <u>click here</u>. To contact us <u>click here</u> or come into our clinic. We will look after you. We will cure you and give you hope for a new life.*

I stared at the page. Everything was there: the address, the phone numbers, even a picture of the clinic. These two "doctors" must have kept Mum's patients there, pretending they were able to cure them. Even

I know there is no cure for AIDS yet. It doesn't mean people have to die. There's no cure for diabetes, either, but there is treatment. AIDS is the same.

I looked back in my black notebook. I remembered Dad telling me about people like this, people who pretend they can cure you by staring into your eyes or giving you little drops of medicine that has nothing in it, only water. He has a name for people like that. There it was, a few pages back in my own handwriting: Snake oil salesmen and charlatans – Dad's description of people who sell cures that don't work.

As I was reading this I realized that we were pulling into Fred's driveway. Nokokulu slammed on the brakes and screeched to a halt, making the car skid into his mum's prize rose bushes. I looked up to see what had happened. There, standing on the driveway waving at us, was Aunt Kiki. She was thinner and paler than the last time we'd seen her, but it was definitely her, and she was smiling.

Nokokulu stared. Almost as if she couldn't believe her eyes.

Fred turned round to me. "It's Aunt Kiki," he whispered. "She's come back."

"I know," I whispered back. I didn't know what else to say. It was like something out of a dream.

Nokokulu reversed the car out of the flower bed

and finally spoke, her voice quieter than usual.

"Chiti, go and say hello to your aunt," she said.

He didn't need a second invitation: he jumped out of the car and ran towards Aunt Kiki. I saw tears in her eyes as she leant down to give him a hug.

"You two," Nokokulu said. "Time to go home now."

Just then Madillo woke up, as if she'd only been having a quick car sleep. "We're back already? That was quick," she said, sitting up.

"Yes," said Nokokulu, opening her door. "It was very quick." She got out of the car and for the first time ever I saw her give someone a hug. She just put her arms around her granddaughter and held onto her tight.

"It's Aunt Kiki," Madillo said, looking at me. "She hasn't disappeared after all. She's here, right here in Fred's garden."

I nodded. It was all too strange. Aunt Kiki appearing out of nowhere, Madillo awake and talking. I needed to get home fast.

BUL-BOO

Ratbag's Wrath

Fred stared at Madillo as we got out of the car.

"You're awake," he said. One of Fred's special skills is stating the obvious.

"Of course I'm awake," Madillo said, laughing. "I'm standing outside the car. You're awake too!"

"We'll see you later, Fred. We'll be back," I said, before the conversation disintegrated any further. "Come, Madillo, let's go." I was impatient to tell Mum and Dad about my discovery and about Aunt Kiki being back.

We crawled through the hedge and came in through the back door. Mum and Dad were sitting at the kitchen table. They both turned to look at us when we came in, and for the first time I understood what peo-

ple mean when they say "the silence was deafening". Neither of them spoke. They just stared at us. Mum with a reproachful look in her eyes and Dad with his deciding-whether-to-be-angry look. Mum's was worse.

Madillo was the first to speak.

"Hi, we're back," she said in a pretending-to-be-chirpy voice.

They both nodded, then looked at one another. Mum tipped her head towards Dad. "You go first."

"OK," he said, taking a deep breath. "Don't ever, *ever* do that again. Never. You want to go somewhere with Fred or with anyone, just ask us. That's all. It's not hard. You both know how to speak. We might say yes, we might say no – but ask us. Instead you lied. Not once, but twice. We don't do that to you. We don't expect it from you. OK? Anything could have happened and we wouldn't have known where you were."

I felt my face burning. Madillo moved closer to me. Neither of us could even look at Mum and Dad.

"And," Mum added, "if it hadn't been for Nokokulu we still wouldn't know."

"Nokokulu?" we both said, surprised.

"Yes, we spoke to her when you were still at Ng'ombe Ilede," Dad explained. "I went next door yesterday evening because Fred's dad had been fishing and he called me over to give me some tilapia. Naturally

I asked where you all were as Mum said she'd spoken to you earlier and you were staying another night. Lie number two. He told me that Fred had gone away with Nokokulu and you had come home yesterday morning."

"So we called Nokokulu," Mum said.

At that we both looked up.

"What?" I said.

"We called her, on her mobile. She told us that you were both with them and she would bring you all back this morning. Although we didn't expect you this early."

Nokokulu on a mobile phone was hard to imagine. And why hadn't we heard it ring?

"Why didn't you phone *me*?" I asked.

"Bul-Boo," Mum said, "your phone was off. And if I were you I wouldn't be asking questions at all right now. I'd be looking down at my feet and saying sorry and promising to never, ever do anything like this again."

Mum in indignant mode is not good; I'm sure she could see we were sorry. Madillo looked as if all she wanted to do was curl up in a ball on the floor and howl.

But then Mum decided to change the subject.

"Bul-Boo, sweetheart," she said, "I've got something to tell you. You remember when you asked me about Ratbag the other day? You must have had some kind of sixth sense."

Madillo looked even more crestfallen. She's always the one trying for a sixth sense. I don't even want one.

"Not a sixth sense, Mum," I said. "Scientific research."

"Whatever it was, you have no idea how important that one little question was. Ratsberg and his partner, both of whom call themselves scientists, have their own theories about AIDS. Well, one theory. They say it doesn't exist. People think all sorts of funny things about this illness and mostly that's OK. But not this. This can lead to murder. Years ago, in South Africa, these two men misinformed the government about this illness. They persuaded certain people they were right, that there was no such thing as HIV or AIDS. Then the government misinformed the people, and as a result no one got proper medicine when they were ill. The disease spread like wildfire. But that's all in the past. South Africa has a new president and things have changed. Instead" – she looked at me and Madillo – "they moved to Zambia. These *hyenas* in their white coats came here to spread their lies and make money promising people health. But you, Bul-Boo, with that one question, helped us to stop that."

I wanted to tell her I already knew that, but Mum was determined not to let me get a word in edgeways.

"So," she continued, "I looked them up, and I found the place and went there yesterday. You don't need to

know the details, but let me tell you that I found Fred's Aunt Kiki and seven other people there. All of them my patients. They had gone downhill very badly, and had all become very thin. Ratbag had them staying there, pumping them full of vitamins, hypnotizing them, getting them to do exercise. And he had them off all their prescribed medicines. He had their heads filled with the idea that he was going to cure them."

"Mum, I also looked it up..." I interrupted.

She waved her hands to let me know that she hadn't finished speaking. When she has something to say it's hard to stop her.

"Can you believe that he had made them all sign 'legal' documents threatening to take them off the *wonderful* holistic cure programme if they came to tell me or their families where they were? I tore up the contracts in front of him. *Professor Ratbag*," she said with vehemence, "Professor Nothing. He's a murderer, plain and simple."

It was hard to take all of this in. It was as I'd thought, sort of, but so much worse. All I could do was nod. I was just relieved that her patients were now safe. Aunt Kiki was back and things were going to be all right.

Madillo turned and whispered in my ear, "And it was you who started it, Bul-Boo." Which was true, but it was nice to hear it from her.

"As of yesterday they're all back on medication," Mum said. "All but two," she corrected herself quietly, looking down at her own shoes for a moment.

Like us, Mum couldn't bear to think about Sonkwe and Thandiwe being dead.

"Will they make it? Will Aunt Kiki?" I asked her.

"They will," Mum said. "I know they will."

Mum never says things she doesn't believe, so that was a relief.

Mum turned towards Dad. "We were just discussing it, your dad and I. I thought we were going to have to take legal action to get the clinic closed, but Dad has spoken to his cousin Sipho. You remember Sipho, girls? The Minister of Transport?"

We nodded.

"Well, he's going to fast-track their expulsion from the country. No one wants them here. They'll be sent packing with their shiny white teeth and bags of tricks."

"The police have already been in contact with Ratsberg advising him of this," Dad added, "and my bet would be that he and Dr Wrath are in the airport as we speak, demanding seats on the next flight out of here."

Mum turned back to us. "So. That's that. Sorry, Bul-Boo, you were saying you'd also looked it up?"

"I did. I found their website."

She grinned. "I was going to say I'd leave it to you

next time but hopefully there never will be a next time." She got up and came to give us both a big hug. "I'm still cross though," she whispered. "No more lies, right?"

We both nodded, which was a little difficult as she was holding us so tightly.

"And," Dad added, "given that you were being driven by Nokokulu I'm mightily relieved you're back in one piece." He laughed. "All the way from here to Ng'ombe Ilede – that's a lot of driving for one tiny witch."

I decided that now would not be a good time to tell them about crashing into the gates at Munda Wanga gardens and just hoped Madillo felt the same. I looked sideways at her. She was smiling to herself.

"You called her a witch, Dad!" she said suddenly.

He winked at her. "A slip of the tongue."

That seemed like a good time to leave, while they were both in such a good mood.

"We'll go over to Fred's to tell him what's happened," I said to them.

"Aunt Kiki has probably told them already," Mum said. "But go across. You can take this to Nokokulu to thank her for bringing you back safely." She handed me a beautiful orange and green *chitenge* cloth. "She can add it to her collection."

Given the choice I might have avoided talking to Nokokulu, but this gave us no option. I suspect that was Mum's plan.

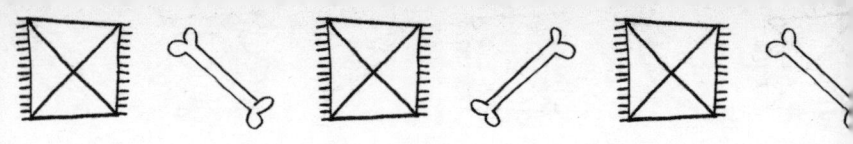

FRED

The Sleep of Forgetting

No one seemed to want to explain anything to me. As if I was just a boy with no brains in my head. And on top of that I had hardly got through the door when Dad started bellowing at me about the twins and their parents, and about me giving Nokokulu a headache. If I gave her a headache, I don't know why she didn't just cast a spell and make it go away again. Surely that would be a pretty simple spell.

After he'd finished telling me off he sent me into the kitchen to join Aunt Kiki and Nokokulu, who were eating breakfast. I didn't feel like eating, mainly because Nokokulu was sitting there with the whole pot of meat in front of her and a giant pile of *nshima* next to it. Great lumps of it were disappearing into her mouth one after the other. I don't know how they all fitted into

her small body. Dad walked past the door and when he looked in he roared with laughter. "It's like watching a snake swallowing rats, isn't it, boy?" Then he went off without waiting for my reply.

At that moment Bul–Boo and Madillo arrived.

"Ha!" Nokokulu said, in between mouthfuls. "*Mpundu!* Come, come inside. You told your parents where you were?"

They just stood there nodding.

"Or did *they* tell *you* where you were?" she said, grinning in that way she does when she thinks she's being especially clever.

They nodded again, staring at her as she went back to devouring her food.

Nokokulu paused in her eating for a moment and looked at Aunt Kiki, who was sitting on the couch, exhausted. "Kiki, my child, do you see these three children in front of me, looking at me like they never saw a hungry person eating before?"

Aunt Kiki said, "Yes, Granny," and gave me a wink.

"Have you ever seen the like before? Answer me that. Three people standing there looking like sheep awaiting slaughter."

Aunt Kiki just laughed.

Nokokulu wiped her fingers and looked at all of us. At Aunt Kiki sitting on the couch, the twins standing in

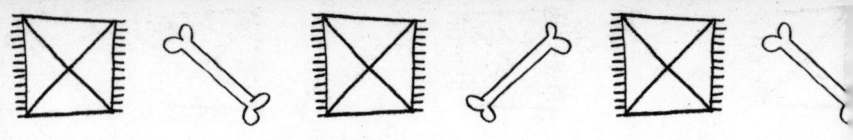

the doorway looking as though they were getting ready to run, and at me sitting right opposite her at the table.

"I'm going to tell you all something," she said. "I am going to say it to you once and then I never want you to talk to anyone about it again. Especially not to me."

I shook my head. "Never, Nokokulu. We'll never speak of it again."

She ignored me and carried on. "I had a child once – Maluba. She was my only daughter. She is still my only child. I know that wherever she is, she still lives in the half-and-half life between now and for ever. She was mother to you, Kiki, and mother to your father, Chiti."

The room had suddenly gone very quiet.

"She was named Maluba for the flower. It was because of her that my grandson married this woman from England who only cares about flowers. Everywhere as far as you can look in her garden there are flowers."

Nokokulu nodded outside to Mum who was trimming a bougainvillea on the front porch.

"You, Chiti boy, you are part of this story. You must learn not to be nosy. If you ask me something, I will tell you. Don't go snooping around in my suitcase like that ever again. You want to know what was inside it? I'll tell you now," she said, and a big fat tear rolled down her cheek. "It was my Maluba's dress. The dress

she wore when she was sixteen – a pretty blue dress with small yellow flowers on it. That's all that was in there. I wanted her with me when I went to seek the Man-Beast."

She looked at me. "Because it was he who took my child. Forty years ago, when your Aunt Kiki and her noisy twin brother were only small babies. Forty years ago, he took her. I had to stop him from doing it again. I had to stop him."

No one said anything.

She wiped the tear away from her cheek. "And now he has been stopped. For ever."

She shook her head. "You can go in a minute, but before you do, let me tell you, Kiki, while you sit there staring at an old woman trying to get a little morsel of food inside her – let me tell you that these three children aren't all bad. These girls were loyal to Chiti and they came with him and me to help rescue you. They will always be welcome in my house."

"Yes," said Aunt Kiki, giving me a small smile.

I didn't know what to say. It was almost easier to deal with nasty Nokokulu, so I just sat there. I watched as Madillo hesitated for a moment and then went over to Nokokulu and put her arms around her neck saying, "And you, Great-grandmother Witch, you are welcome in my house any day too."

Nokokulu coughed loudly then said, "Good child, good child," before shoving in another mouthful.

"And this is for you," Bul-Boo added, handing over the *chitenge* she'd been holding. "From Mum, to say thank you for bringing us home safely."

"Ha!" said Nokokulu, which I suppose could be interpreted as a thank you. "Now, off you go, children. Go and play those silly computer games that shrivel up your brains." But there was definitely a glimmer of a smile in her eyes as she said it.

As we all headed off, she called me back, saying to the twins, "You, *mpundu*, you go upstairs. I need to tell Chiti one more thing."

When they had gone she beckoned me to her and whispered, "The little one, Mad Girl, she will not remember anything that happened. She has been given the Sleep of Forgetting. I don't want you telling her anything. You hear me? Nothing."

She then shooed me out of the kitchen.

I ran upstairs to join the twins and when I got into the room I shut the door carefully behind me.

"What did she want?" Bul-Boo asked.

"Just to tell me that I'm still her favourite great-grandson," I said.

"She could have said that in front of us. Everyone knows that," Madillo said. "What did she really say?"

216

"Exactly that. 'Fred, you're my favourite great-grandson.'"

I wondered how long I would have to keep this up.

"So, she called you Fred?" Bul-Boo asked suspiciously.

"When she's in a good mood she does." OK, time to change the subject now. "But that doesn't matter anyway. Did you hear what she said about my grand-mother, that she was taken by the Man-Beast? As if that wasn't bad enough, when she thought the Man-Beast was returning, forty years later, she took us with her to find him, endangering our lives and our souls."

"Well, we're all right now," Madillo said. "So noth-ing was really endangered, and I liked being there. Plus she brought great food."

Bul-Boo and I looked at her. This wasn't like Madillo at all. Surely she'd want to talk about the Man-Beast.

"Do you remember anything about what happened when you went to cover up the hyena footprints?" Bul-Boo asked, before I could stop her.

A grin appeared on Madillo's face. "The only reason I went to wipe them away was so I could leave the two of you alone for a bit…"

For that she got a sharp whack across the arm from Bul-Boo.

I didn't know where to look.

"OK, OK, that wasn't really the reason," Madillo

said, laughing. "I went to wipe the paw prints away and for some reason I felt really, really tired, so I lay down just for a bit and must have fallen asleep."

She frowned. "I did fall asleep, now I remember: I had weird dreams about the two-legged hyena. It must have been because we'd been talking about it. There was someone else who came into the dream too. A really tall man who looked like one of those beautiful carvings. You know, the ones that are just skinny the whole way up and down and have beads on their necks and legs and everywhere?"

We both nodded.

It was true what Nokokulu had said – Madillo really didn't know that this had actually happened.

"The man in my dream looked like that. Anyway, then I woke up back in the car." She looked surprised at this, as if it had only just occurred to her how odd this was. "Who put me in there?" She wrinkled her nose. "I hope you didn't carry me, Fred?"

I couldn't see why that thought would cause anyone to wrinkle their nose up.

"No," Bul-Boo said. "It was a man who looked like that, like the man you're describing. Somehow Nokokulu knows him. She went out to look for you because we couldn't find you, and when she came back he was with her, carrying you."

Madillo stared at us. "Stop it, Bul-Boo! How could a man who appeared in my dreams pick me up without me waking?"

I didn't know how to make Bul-Boo stop talking so I went behind Madillo's back and tried to signal to her to keep quiet. The only problem was that Madillo saw my reflection in the window and turned round.

"What's the matter with the two of you?" she shouted, sounding on the verge of tears. "Just tell me! What's going on?"

Bul-Boo finally got the message.

"Sorry, Madillo," she said quickly. "It's not true. There was no man. It was Nokokulu who carried you to the car. She's stronger than she looks. She said you stayed asleep because you were exhausted from all the noise you'd been making."

"But there was a two-legged hyena," I said, before I could stop myself.

At that they both turned on me.

"What?"

I probably shouldn't have blurted that out, but this wasn't the part Nokokulu had told me to keep quiet about. And as I was the only one who had seen it I decided it was OK to carry on.

"We were driving away, you were both asleep, and the car hit something. It made a kind of thudding noise

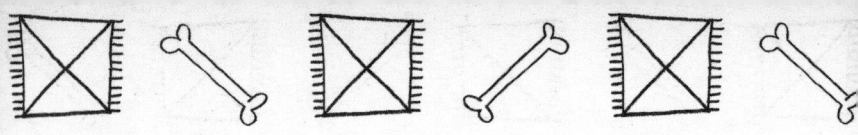

as if we'd knocked someone over. I asked Nokokulu if I should get out and look in case we had killed someone, or an animal or something. But she said no. In fact she said she didn't care what it was as long as her car was all right. Even if it was a baby." (That was an exaggeration, but you cannot tell a good story without exaggerating.) "So we drove off and I looked behind us and do you know what I saw?"

"No."

"A giant animal, bigger than a lion but not quite as big as an elephant. It was lying there as if it was dead. Then suddenly it lifted its head up and it stared at me. Stared right at me with yellow eyes. It was as if it knew me."

Mum says I have a condition called confabulation – where I fill in details where there is supposed to be nothing. So if it's a story about a horse galloping through a town and coming out the other side without incident, by the time I tell it the horse will have had seventeen extraordinary experiences along the way. Maybe she's right.

"Did it stand up?" Madillo asked.

"No. After it lifted its head it lay down in a weak, dead kind of way. And I couldn't see much as Nokokulu wanted to get away and it was dark. I couldn't even see how many legs it had."

"Fred, are you making this up?" Bul-Boo asked suspiciously.

"No! I couldn't make something like that up," I said.

"Well, you could," Madillo argued. "We all know that."

She was right. I probably could.

"You know, Fred," said Bul-Boo, "it could have been a stray dog from Pambazana village. A really big dog that wandered off and happened to get in the way of Nokokulu and her yellow car."

"It could," I conceded, "but it also could have been a two-legged hyena. A Man-Beast. Couldn't it?"

She shrugged, as she does when she doesn't want to admit that I could be right.

The three of us sat looking at one another for a few moments until I jumped up and said, "I challenge whoever of you is first downstairs to a game of Ultimate Tenkaichi."

We all ran down to the playroom and managed to spend the next hour on the PlayStation, miraculously uninterrupted by parents, small irritating younger brothers or great-grandparents. That was a first.

Bul-Boo and I played against each other and Madillo sat next to us giving a running commentary.

The three of us together. As it should be.

Epilogue

The tall man runs slowly in the moonlight, his steps even and steady. He will run like this until he reaches his home.

As he runs he thinks about the beast who roamed this earth since time began: a creature who outlived the hunters, the traders, the farmers and the fishermen; a creature who kept to himself, and hid behind the smallest of rocks or up in the tallest of trees; a creature whose size changed in the moonlight.

He has seen him too many times to count.

And now he is gone. For ever. His footprints will no longer frighten the people who come here seeking answers from those who have gone before them; he will no longer prey on those who venture out of their villages.

The man thinks about the old woman, the one who has no fear in her, not of the living or the dead. She is a mystery to him. He had not seen her before, yet he felt that he knew her. On her face were the lines of those who lived long ago.

It was she who ended the reign of the ancient creature.

It was she who blessed the small girl with the sleep of forgetting.

As he runs he knows he will not be able to forget the old woman. He cannot, for she has freed him from his burden of following the creature who has no name; the burden of trying to protect those he would attack; and most of all the burden of failure.

He watched as the young girl crept out of the small tent; watched as she walked fearfully to where the creature had been. Then he saw the eyes, the greedy yellow eyes. They were also watching.

The yellow eyes moved away from the girl and stared at the man. The man stared back, feeling the waves of hopelessness flood through him.

Then the beast started walking slowly and quietly towards the young girl, with the strange gait of one who should have four legs but now has only two. He rolled as he walked, his body awkward and clumsy, his small withered arms held in front of his face.

The young girl looked up as the shadow fell across her. She stood perfectly still, frozen to the ground. She did not scream. The beast leant down and scooped her into his arms. The tall man had seen this before. He knew that when the fear was this big all else stopped.

Now was the time. It was always this way.

The tall man came and stood in front of the beast. He no longer feared him, because he knew it was not him that the beast wanted. He had stood before him like this many times. Sometimes he had saved those that the beast preyed upon; more times he had failed.

"Leave this one. Leave her. Let her return to her family."

The beast held the young girl tighter and laughed, a howling rough laugh that bounced off the trees.

The tall man's heart beat faster.

The beast did not move.

The tall man knew this trick. Once before he had walked forward to try and grab the prey away, but the beast had been quicker than he was. In the blink of an eye he had opened his wide jaws and snapped them shut over his victim. The tall man had never walked forward again.

Just then he heard a sound behind him and turned round.

A tiny old woman was standing there. The tiny old

woman who he now thinks of as he runs towards his home.

"Ha!" she said, pointing at the beast. "You, put that child down. Now."

The beast laughed again.

A small grin appeared on the old woman's face.

"Laughing Hyena, you think that frightens me? Two-legged Hyena, you think that frightens me? You do not know me, but after today you will not laugh again."

The beast opened his mouth, but instead of laughter a swarm of buzzing honey bees flew out. An endless swarm that seemed to glow in the night. They landed on every part of him, his eyes, his nose, his ears. Some turned around and flew back into his open mouth.

The tall man watched as the beast twitched and turned with each sting.

"Laugh now, you two-legged cowardly runt of a creature, laugh now!" the old woman said, hopping back and forth from one leg to another.

Suddenly the buzzing stopped and the bees turned, as one, and disappeared into the night.

"Give me the girl now," the old woman instructed.

The beast looked at her, silently, his legs trembling.

"Ha!" the old woman said, and the beast slowly collapsed, falling softly to the ground.

The tall man ran forward and grabbed the young girl from his little stunted arms. A cloud of dust rose up around the beast and a strangled breath came out of his swollen mouth.

The young girl looked up at the man who now held her, her eyes wide with fear.

"Come here," the old woman told him. "Put her down on the ground."

The tall man did as he was told and placed her gently down. The old woman leant over her and softly ran her fingers over her eyes. They closed.

"The Sleep of Forgetting," the old woman whispered. "It will wipe all this from her mind."

Then the tall man lifted her up again and took her to where the old woman led him.

He knows she is safe now, the small one and her sister who looks no different from her. Safe and at home.

The tall man stops running. He has reached the banks of the Kariba Dam. He sits down on the soft shore and stares out over the shining expanse of water, his heart filled with gladness.

For the first time in centuries he can rest his weary body.

For the first time in centuries he has nothing to fear. His task is complete. He too will sleep, and forget.

Leabharlanna Poibli Chathair Baile Átha Cliath
Dublin City Public Libraries

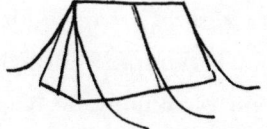

Thanks and acknowledgements

As with *The Butterfly Heart*, lots of people played a part in this book's arrival. Thanks first, as always, to Tom, Amy, Christie, Kate, Aisling and Maurice and to my extended family, every single one of them. They know who they are – in-laws, out-laws, nephews, nieces, cousins, aunts and uncles. It is said that you can choose your friends but you can't choose your family: given the choice I would change nothing.

A special thanks this time to Orla Mackey in Kilkenny. Orla did the teaching notes for *The Butterfly Heart* and *The Sleeping Baobab Tree*. She is, to my mind, the kind of teacher that all teachers should be – kind, curious, hard-working, creative, insightful and patient. Thank you, Orla.

Many other people are due thanks for their role in

this book and their support of *The Butterfly Heart*: my lovely writers' group, the Crabapples: Jean, Gemma, Una and Geoff; Siobhán Parkinson; Vukani Nyirenda at Kalimatundu Tales; John Nchimunyality Cargula; Mwanabibi Sikamo at Uprooting the Pumpkin; Bwalya Chileya; Mary Esther Judy; Mpikeleni Duma; Karabo Kgoleng; the Phiri family in Lusaka; Colleen Cailin Jones; Elaina O'Neill; Rachel Leydon; the Coopoo family; Marian Oliver; Louie Calvert; Alice Bennett; Stephanie Meaney; Brian Roche and St John's School; Daniel Sana and Sydney Chibbabbuka of Bantu Pathfinders; my young writers' group in the Kilkenny Tech; CBI and *Inis* for their fantastic support of children's literature; the judges who awarded me the Éilís Dillon Award; SCBWI for their work in promoting children's books; the libraries, the wonderful libraries, we are privileged to have them; the Kilkenny bookshops – we are blessed in Kilkenny with great bookshops and they have been a fantastic support; and all the other bookshops around the country. And to anyone else I may have forgotten ... sorry! Any omissions I will make good on my website at www.thebutterflyheart.net, I promise.

Special thanks due...

To Sophie Hicks, still a Wonder Woman amongst agents, and to Edina Imrik and all the staff at Ed Victor; to Emma Lidbury and Gill Evans at Walker Books, both truly gifted editors, for once again showing faith in my writing; to Gillian Hibbs (at www.gillianhibbs.co.uk) and Maria Soler Canton for the beautiful artwork and cover design; to Conor Hackett and everyone else at Walker Books, a magical publisher.

And finally...

This book, like *The Butterfly Heart*, is set in Zambia. As my childhood home it lingers long in my memory, may it flourish and grow.

Nsolo and Mancala

In the book, Fred, Bul-Boo and Madillo play a game called *nsolo* while they're trying to pass the time at Ng'ombe Ilede. Unfortunately for the twins Fred always wins – perhaps because he was trained by his great-grandmother, who as we well know is something of a witch.

Nsolo is a game that can be played anywhere by making holes in the ground and using small stones or seeds, which is how the twins and Fred play it. It is played all over Africa and goes by different names in different countries: you can now buy a version of it called *mancala*, which uses a wooden board and marbles. It's great for improving your maths skills while having fun – perhaps persuade your teachers to get a board for your classroom!

The version of the game played in Zambia is very complicated. If you would like to learn it you could look up the rules in Professor Mwizenge Tembo's book *Satisfying Zambian Hunger for Culture*, which is invaluable for anyone wishing to learn more about this wonderful country. If you go to www.infobarrel.com and type into the search box the word *"nsolo"* you will find his article on it.

If you manage to get hold of a *mancala* board the rules are different, and the game (which looks like the picture below) will have a set of rules with it. *Mancala* can be played from about five years and upwards and is great fun.

Amnesty International

The story of *The Sleeping Baobab Tree* is partly about our human rights, including the right to medical help, to enjoy our own culture, and to freedom of belief and freedom of expression.

We all have human rights, no matter who we are or where we live. Human rights are part of what makes us human. They help us to live lives that are fair and truthful, free from abuse, fear and want and respectful of other people's rights. But they are often abused and we need to stand up for them.

Amnesty International is a movement of ordinary people from across the world standing up for humanity and human rights. Our purpose is to protect individuals wherever justice, fairness, freedom and truth are denied.

To find out more about human rights and how to start one of our very active Amnesty youth groups, go to www.amnesty.org.uk/youth

To find out about how you can use fiction to teach human rights in the classroom, go to www.amnesty.org.uk/education

Amnesty International UK, The Human Rights Action Centre
17–25 New Inn Yard, London EC2A 3EA   020 7033 1500
www.amnesty.org.uk

"Amnesty's greetings cards really helped me in prison. In total, I received more than 4,000 – amazing! I read each one: the best, I think, were those from children and other student activists... It amazed me to see that those children know about human rights. What a good omen for the future!"

Ignatius Mahendra Kusuma Wardhana, *an Indonesian student who was arrested at a peaceful demonstration in 2003 and spent two years, seven months and ten days behind bars, where he was beaten and threatened.*

To download full teacher's notes on
The Sleeping Baobab Tree and *The Butterfly Heart,* go to:

www.walker.co.uk/downloads

and scroll down to the **Age 9+** section.

Or, if you have a smart phone, scan the codes below:

The Butterfly Heart   *The Sleeping Baobab Tree*
Teacher's notes   Teacher's notes

"Ifwafwa. Yes, that's what they call me. The
Puff Adder. Slow and heavy, but fast to strike."

Bul-Boo and Madillo are powerless to save their
friend Winifred from a terrifying fate, and
time is slipping away. In desperation they call
upon Ifwafwa, the snake man. But although
the man is wise, he is slow and the girls become
impatient. Will he strike before it's too late?

A lyrical story from
the butterfly heart of Africa.

MICHAEL MORPURGO
RODDY DOYLE
PATRICIA McCORMICK
THERESA BRESLIN
DAVID ALMOND
URSULA DUBOSARSKY
MALORIE BLACKMAN
SARAH MUSSI
JAMILA GAVIN
EOIN COLFER
MARGARET MAHY
IBTISAM BARAKAT
MEJA MWANGI
RITA WILLIAMS-GARCIA

FREE?

STORIES CELEBRATING
HUMAN RIGHTS

ONE UNIVERSAL DECLARATION PROCLAIMS 30 RIGHTS AND FREEDOMS FOR EVERYBODY.

But 60 years on, millions of people around
the world are still denied full human rights.

14 acclaimed storytellers take inspiration from
their struggle.

All royalties from the sale of this book go to Amnesty International,
which works to protect human rights all over the world.

A tale of dreams
and midsummer magic.

Masha lives in Icarus, the abandoned trolleybus,
until one stormy night when he takes off,
transporting her to an enchanted place where
Cossacks dance and tigers roar. It's nearly
midsummer's eve, when she can make a wish for
her heart's desire. But will Masha make the right
wish, enabling herself and her mother to escape
Uncle Igor's clutches and live happily ever after?